MEMOIRS OF A PIANO

MEMOIRS OF A PIANO

A Whimsical Adventure

Kyra Petrovskaya Wayne

To order additional copies of this book, contact:
Xlibris Corporation
1-888-795-4274
www.Xlibris.com
Orders@Xlibris.com
37350

BOOKS
by Kyra Petrovskaya Wayne

Kyra
An Autobiography,
Prentice-Hall, 1959,
Quest For The Golden Fleece
Lothrop, Lee and Shepard, 1960
Kyra's Secrets Of Russian Cooking
Prentice-Hall, 1961,
Shurik, A story Of The Siege of Leningrad
Grosset and Dunlap, 1970
The Awakening
Grosset and Dunlap, 1973
The Witches Of Barguzin
Thomas Nelson, 1975
Rekindle The Dreams
Dale, 1977
Max, The Dog That Refused To Die
Alpine Publications,1979
Quest For Empire, A Saga Of Russian America
Hancock House Publishers, 1986
Li'l Ol' Charlie
Alpine Publications, 1989
Quest For Bigfoot
Hancock House Publishers, 1996
Pepper's Ordeal
Hancock House Publishers, 2000
The Chaperone
Trafford Publishing, 2006

PRELUDE

After more than fifty years of knocking about Europe and Russia, I will be celebrating my *Golden Anniversary* on American shores. I hope you will find this chronicle enlightening, and even though my language is a little old-fashioned, I am sure you will forgive me. After all, I am a hundred years old.

Allow me to introduce myself. My ancestry dates back to the Middle Ages. My immediate family tree has its roots in the eighteenth century, sprouting forth into many branches and still growing. I am fruitwood-brown, but many of my brothers and cousins, who are scattered around the world, are ebony-black, or mahogany-red, or even ivory-white.

I have a set of eighty-eight splendid teeth, thirty-six of which are made of ebony. The remaining fifty-two are made of ivory. In this respect I have something in common with George Washington: he, too, supposed to have had teeth made of ivory.

I am elegant, although my legs are a bit thick. They have to be, for I am rather hefty and it requires at least two men to move me around. I have changeable heartbeat, from *staccato* to very sensual *legato,* produced by dozens of small hammers, but do not worry. I am very healthy.

By now you must have guessed who I am. I am a piano. My name is *Pleyel*, and I am French. I made my decision to record my memoirs upon hearing a young piano student exclaim, "If only pianos could talk! What marvelous tales would they tell us!"

Well, here it is, my tale, the story of my *first hundred years*.

ONE

I was very young when I was first introduced to the public. I was shiny and eager to please everyone, never yet having been put on public display. I felt shy as I stood in the center of a beautifully appointed Salon on the most fashionable street in Paris, the Avenue de Champs d'Élysée. There were two other pianos and a golden harp in the Salon, ready to be touched and plucked and played, for only then could we demonstrate our incomparable tone to our prospective customers.

Although the harp was made in Italy and the pianos came from Germany, we, true cosmopolitans, had no trouble in communicating with one another. We conversed easily by means of our symbols. How often since then had I thought what might have happened to music if its symbols, or notes had been different in each country. An Italian would not have been able to play the Russian music of Tchaikovsky or a Frenchman the music of Bach, or a German the music of Debussy. They all would have had to know one another's language or be limited to their own national composers. As it was, we were lucky that someone, centuries ago, invented the universal system of musical writing.

My first day at the Salon proved to be very exciting. I was touched and played by half a dozen people, who were considering buying me. I tried my best to look brave, smiling broadly with all my eighty-eight teeth, but trembling inwardly and even vibrating my strings from sheer nervousness. I hoped that no one had noticed it. I wanted to make a good impression.

However, I did not want to be sold on my first day out. I wanted to get acclimated to my image as a *piano*, and not a conglomeration of strings, pedals, wood boards, and lids. I wanted to enjoy the admiration of the customers and to hear their exclamations of pleasure when they touched me and I responded with full sonorous sound.

Alas, on my very first day I was chosen over my two German cousins. I heard our proprietor Monsieur Duval, extolling my virtues, telling the customers that they would never regret buying me. I was the best to be had. After all, I was a *Pleyel*, the piano *adored* by our Empress Eugenie. I heard my

German cousins sigh with envy. They groaned and protested, for they were unfortunate enough to be exposed to the rough pounding of the customer who insisted on trying all of us.

My new masters fascinated me. There were three of them. Monsieur de Matignon, a tall, well-dressed man with a carefully tended beard, touched with gray and his wife, a plump, handsome woman. According to my friend, the Italian harp, who had traveled around the world and was aware of the trends in fashion and thought, Madame de Matignon was dressed in the latest fashion. But the third member of the family, the daughter, was the most exquisite creature I had ever seen. Of course, until then, I had met very few women. Once or twice I saw the wife and daughter of my builder, but they failed to impress me either with their looks or with their manners. They poked at my teeth with their fingers, and they stepped on my pedals as if I were a pebble under their feet and had no feeling. I did not like them. But, this lovely creature, Mademoiselle Solange, captivated my heart immediately. When she ran her slender fingers over my keys, for this is really what my teeth are called, I sang with joy, giving my all to her gentle, caressing touch.

She had her eyes only for me. "I *love* this piano!" she cried. "Please, Papa, buy it for me!"

Needless to say, Monsieur Matignon bought me and personally supervised my placement on a special wagon, pulled by two strong horses. My legs were unscrewed and several layers of special padding encircled my body. I thought, how fortunate it was that my legs could be so easily separated from my body, without any pain or after-affects. Imagine, Monsieur Matignon with *his* legs unscrewed?

The horses pulled the heavy wagon along the Champs d'Élysée at a stately, slow pace. Although I was resting on my side, I was able to observe a few sights of Paris.

The avenue was full of strolling people, dressed in high fashion, very much like my new masters. I saw a handsome open carriage pulled by four white horses pass in the opposite direction. A beautiful, auburn-haired woman in a small hat with a gossamer veil was seated on the crimson cushions of the carriage. I instantly recognized Empress Eugenie, the wife of Napoleon III, our national leader, for her portrait adorned the wall of Monsieur Duval's music Salon. "Her Majesty *adores* Pleyel pianos," the words of the proprietor came to my mind.

The Empress smiled and made small gestures of greeting with her gloved hand toward her subjects. Her carriage was accompanied by a group of young guards on horseback, resplendent in their bright gold-braided uniforms, their swords reflecting the sun. The Empress passed by my wagon, looking at me with interest, perhaps recognizing me as a *"Pleyel,"* but soon I lost her from the orbit of my vision.

There were other things to observe on this splendid day. I saw children play under tall chestnut trees supervised by their uniformed nannies. I saw young men promenading slowly, watching the ladies from the corner of their eyes and I saw the ladies, of course! There were hundreds of lovely ladies riding in the carriages pulled by well-groomed horses or strolling slowly under the trees. Some of them held in their arms strange little creatures that did not look like children, yet the ladies talked to them with endearing terms, as if they were children. These strange creatures made quaint noises, very unpleasant to my highly critical music senses. If only my friend, the Italian harp were here! She would have known what those creatures were!

It did not take me long, to make an acquaintance with one of these creatures. My new mistress, Solange, had one. The creatures were dogs.

From the moment we met, the dog and I knew that we disliked one another. Frou-Frou, for this was his name, greeted me at the door of the Matignon house with shrill, hysterical barks. Solange tried to stop him, but instead of smacking him, she picked him up and *kissed* him! Really!

But the worst came later, when the workmen assembled all my parts and moved me onto a little stage at the bay window in the salon.

I commanded the room. The rest of the furniture immediately acknowledged my dominance by faint creaking, discernable only by me, due to my exceptional sensitivity to sound.

Solange seated herself on a special round stool that came with me from the music Salon, and touched my keys with her gentle fingers. Immediately the little beast, Frou-Frou, lifted his head up and uttered such an earsplitting howl that everyone but I broke up in laughter. The more Solange played, the louder the little monster howled.

"Let's lock him up, Maman," Solange finally said. "Obviously Frou-Frou doesn't appreciate music." She picked up the dog, but instead of punishing him for his disgraceful behavior, she petted him and handed him to a maid, who took the squirming creature away. I sighed with relief, but I knew that from then on, I had a rival for Solange's affections and a constant enemy.

As months passed by, my passion for Solange continued to increase. She was very musical and I, who had never been played yet by anyone but the tuners and the master builders at the factory, thought that she was the best pianist in the world. But then, Franz Liszt honored me by his divine touch.

I heard from our maids, that my masters were going to give a musical Soirée. The grand salon was thoroughly dusted. Three highly trained specialists, who wore soft brushes on their feet, polished the parquet floors by making peculiar, ice-skating movements, shuffling all over the house until the floors shone like my own lid. The florists delivered baskets of fragrant flowers while the housemaids scattered around the house polishing silver candelabras and crystal chandeliers. My own insides full of little hammers and strings were inspected, dusted and tuned by my former friend and owner Monsieur Duval, the proprietor of the music Salon.

Finally, everything was ready for the gala evening. I was in good spirits, anticipating the forthcoming party with great excitement. The famous Hungarian composer and virtuoso, Franz Liszt, was going to be the guest of honor and play his compositions.

Franz Liszt! To have the great master touch my keys! It was beyond my imagination. I suddenly felt nervous.

I observed that Solange and her parents were nervous also. For once little yapping Frou-Frou was locked up unceremoniously in Solange's bedroom without so much as a pat on his silly fluffy head with its stupid pink bow.

Solange's mother entered the salon for a last minute inspection. She wore a diamond necklace and earrings and was dressed in a magnificent lilac-colored velvet gown. She smelled of jasmine and her bare shoulders glowed with white powder. She ran her gloved fingers over my keys in search of hidden dust but there was none. The maids were well trained in our household.

Then, my love Solange entered, accompanied by her father. She looked adorable in a white lace dress, with a corsage of tiny pink roses at her narrow waist. She wore the similar pink roses in her long blond hair and she was surrounded by a faint scent of roses. Her hands and arms were covered with long white kid gloves. She, too, examined my keyboard, my lid and found everything to her satisfaction. Meanwhile, her father walked among the rows of elegant gold chairs, which were arranged in a semi-circle around me, so that every guest would have a good, unobstructed view of the artist and the piano, that is, *me!*

As the butler announced the first arrivals, my masters went to receive their guests at the foot of the marble staircase.

Soon the salon was full of laughter and chatter. The guests sipped champagne served to them by the maids. The majestic butler carried a huge silver tray crowded with tall crystal goblets, but everyone kept glancing at the door, waiting for the guest of honor. I heard it mentioned that it was a rare honor indeed, when the great Maestro agreed to play at a private party. It was said that Liszt came to Paris very seldom now, living most of the time in Weimar, Germany and that only his friendship with my master made him forsake the seclusion of his study for a private concert. Some of the guests doubted whether Liszt could still perform, remembering him as a young, incomparable, fiery virtuoso of a quarter of a century ago. The others snickered that Liszt probably needed a lot of money to support his mistress, Madame d'Agoult, and so had to give a private concert because of it.

The more I listened to the gossip of the guests, the more challenged I felt. I decided that the least I could do, was to help the grand old man put on a great performance, such as had never been heard before.

There was a commotion at the door and a hush fell upon the festive crowd. The great Maestro had arrived.

From my vantage point on the little stage, I could see a tall, thin man, leaning heavily on the arm of my master. The Maestro's hair was almost white, parted in the middle, falling loosely on his slightly stooped shoulders. He was attired in the black priestly robes that he wore as a member of St. Francis of Assisi, a religious order he joined a few years before. He must have been a very handsome man in his youth, for even now he was a striking figure.

He walked toward me, and placing one hand on the corner of my case, bowed ceremoniously to his audience. Then he seated himself on the stool and folded his hands as if in a prayer. I have never seen such long, thin fingers. He flexed them and they moved like so many-jointed talons of some mythical majestic bird. He lifted his leonine head, his eyes shut, his lips slightly parted, and struck the first chord of his *Hungarian Rhapsody #2*, the most popular of his Rhapsodies as I was to learn later.

I responded with all my heart. Forgive the cliché, dear readers, but even though I am an inanimate object, a mere piano, I *insist* that I possess a heart. How else could I move your human emotions so deeply, if I myself did not have a feeling, pulsating heart?

As the old Maestro began his second selection, the *Mephisto Waltz,* which he had written for the orchestra, but sometimes performed as a piano piece, his countenance suddenly became Mephistophelean, the corners of his mouth curving in a sardonically-devilish expression, only to change to sweet and dreamy one during his rendition of the heart-breaking *Liebesträume.*

Each of his selections received bursts of applause from his audience. He was used to adulation. For more than fifty years he had been the undisputed master of the piano. Finally, Liszt stood up, his face pale from exhaustion. "No more" he said softly. "I am tired." Monsieur Matignon quickly came to his side with a glass of wine. Liszt drank it thirstily and his spirits revived considerably.

"This is a fine instrument, *mon ami,*" he said to my master, stroking my side. "I made my debut on one just like this one. My old friend Chopin always insisted on *Pleyel* for his concerts. He called it *'the ultimate French piano'.*"

I swelled with pride. To hear the great virtuoso's praise filled me with indescribable joy.

The guests, one by one, thanked the Maestro for his divine music. Liszt looked tired and, I thought, bored. He had heard all these compliments before. At last my love, Solange, had pity on him.

"Monsieur Liszt," she said sweetly, "may I accompany you for a little supper?" Liszt took her arm and she led him out of the salon. The guests followed.

I was sorry to part with the Maestro, but I knew that the old man was in good hands. He was with my Solange.

"He must have been so handsome when he was young!" I heard a lady exclaim, looking with adoration at the departing composer.

"He was, indeed," said my master and lowering his voice, added, "Did you know my dear, that it was Franz Liszt who began the tradition of lifting the lid of the piano and sitting in profile to the public during his performances? He was well aware of the devastating power his handsome profile had on the fair ladies in the audience!" Everyone laughed, but I wanted to shout, "Don't you understand, you fools, that *acoustically it is necessary?* The lifted lid throws the sound right at the audience! Thus, a pianist *must* sit in the profile!" But of course, my mute protest had no effect on my master or on his guests.

I never saw Franz Liszt again, but even now, more than a hundred years later, I am proud that once upon a time, the great virtuoso and I had made heavenly music together. I think that no one is still around to make such a claim.

TWO

After Franz Liszt's concert my life of contentment in the Matignon household changed dramatically. Solange became intimidated by the great virtuoso's performance, acutely aware of the insignificance of her own ability. She abandoned me. It was rather silly of her, for no one could be compared to Liszt, probably not even Chopin. But such was her strange logic that she stopped coming to the salon, as if this room reminded her too painfully of her own musical inadequacy.

I spent my days in boredom. Although I saw Solange very seldom now, unfortunately that was not the case with Frou-Frou. The wretched little creature developed a ghastly habit of sneaking into the salon and lifting his leg against my intricately carved extremity! He was too lazy to ask the maids to let him out into the garden. What a beast! I suffered the indignity in silence, although my strings would tighten to a point when I feared they would snap.

Life was becoming unbearable. In my unexpected solitude I began to look forward to the boisterous visits of the maids who invaded the salon twice a week to dust and to clean. They were robust country girls whose healthy vitality pleased me. I liked when one of them would poke on my keyboard a lively tune and sing a bawdy peasant song. But that was a rare occasion. Mostly, I had to satisfy myself by eavesdropping on their gossip.

The maids worried about the approaching war with Prussia. They had sweethearts and brothers, who would be called for military service should war be declared. According to the girls, there seemed to be a disagreement between France and Prussia as to who was to occupy the throne of *Spain*. Prussia wanted to place one of her princes on the vacant Spanish throne, while France, quite naturally, objected. If anyone bothered to seek *my* opinion, I would have advised Prussia and France to stay out of Spanish affairs. Let the Spaniards put one of their own on their throne. They should certainly find someone, I would have said. As it was—no one asked for my opinion. Of course, to you, it might seem to be sheer insanity to ask a *piano* for an opinion, but I must confess, I have always thought of myself to be one of you, you know, a person.

And so, a terrible chain of events started to unroll. The French Emperor Napoleon III, the husband of my admirer, Eugenie, declared war against Prussia. It led to a disaster, ended by his downfall. But I am getting ahead of my story.

The Matignon household was full of weeping women now. All the sweethearts and brothers of our maids were conscripted into the army. Even the Matignon family did not escape the calamity. My angel, Solange, had a brother, who was called to the colors directly from his Military Academy in St.Cyr. The family went to see him off. I heard my master declare he was proud that his son was going to defend the honor of his country. I still could not understand why *the honor of France* had to be defended while the argument was about *Spain,* but such were the intricacies of international politics.

Solange and her mother walked around with their eyes rimmed in red from constant weeping, while my master seemed to be revitalized by the news of war, in which he did not have to fight, but which provided him with a vicarious feeling of participation. He spread a huge map of Europe on the floor in the salon and amused himself by following the movements of French and Prussian armies by sticking little colorful flags on the map.

The tempo of life in our household picked up considerably. Although Solange still refused to play the piano, at least the family spent their evenings in my company, watching my master play with his little flags while the ladies occupied themselves doing needlepoint.

Then a disaster struck. The war was lost. So were the provinces of Alsace and Lorraine, which were annexed by Prussia. To add to the disaster, our Emperor, Napoleon III, surrendered on the battlefield to the Prussians.

Immediately the streets of Paris filled with thousands of rioting citizens demanding that Napoleon III abdicate. On September the fourth, 1870, the Royal family fled Paris to finish their days in exile and the Republic was proclaimed.

But the war continued. Before I was able to sort out my impressions, the Matignon family was leaving Paris for their country estate. Their son was among thousands of prisoners taken by the Prussians, his fate for the time being unknown. Monsieur Matignon expected civil disturbances, perhaps even a revolution, and decided to wait out in the country until the dust of rebellion settled over Paris. No one thought of me. The family departed with their servants, leaving only an old caretaker and his wife to look after the house. My heart was breaking as I heard the carriages pull away from the courtyard, taking my darling Solange out of my life. She did not even come to say good-bye, but she did not forget that horrid little Frou-Frou! She carried him tenderly in her arms.

If I were a human being, I would have wept. I had a premonition that I would never see Solange again.

The Matignons left none too soon. The victorious Prussians surrounded Paris, blockading the city and subjecting its citizens to starvation and death. Our house was left in complete darkness. The old caretaker shuffled through it once a day and his footsteps were the only sounds that would awaken me from my imposed slumber. I reached the point when I lost all sense of time and did not know, or cared whether it was night or day. At first I counted the hours, as the bronze clock on the mantle kept chiming. But after a week the clock needed rewinding. No one cared, and the clock stopped. In my solitary existence, I began to long even for Frou-Frou. At least he was alive and one could hate him.

One morning I was awakened by the hurried footsteps of the caretaker and his wife. Breathing heavily, they ran into the salon and threw open the heavy draperies. The brilliant light of the morning made me wince. I became accustomed to complete darkness and the sight of sun and cloudless sky almost blinded me. As I acclimated myself to the light, I looked beyond the bay window. Every building was sharply outlined against the cold deep blue of the sky. I could clearly see every hue, from dark green to bright yellow on the trees underneath our windows. I breathed in deeply the invigorating autumn air as the caretaker flung open the double doors leading to the balcony. He and his wife leaned against the railing, their faces uplifted, as if they were watching something in the sky. Curiosity made me follow their stares.

I saw a strange, round object, which reminded me of a ball that Frou-Frou used to play with and carry in his mouth. It was huge and was painted in many bright colors. It had a wicker basket suspended under it by stout ropes and I could clearly see two men standing in the basket, holding the ropes. The ball was drifting slowly with the wind.

"How do you like it! Some rats are escaping from Paris in the balloon!" exclaimed the caretaker's wife. She sounded envious.

"That's what it is! It is a *balloon*!" I thought. I had heard my master discuss with his friends this new invention that made it possible to fly through the air like a bird. It seemed incredible. At the time, I dismissed the whole idea as a mere fantasy, but here it was, floating high in the sky, growing smaller and smaller, until it disappeared from view.

"I wonder who are they?" the caretaker's wife continued. "They must be very brave fellows to use this contraption!"

"Yes, very brave or very foolish ones," laughed the caretaker. "If the balloon doesn't explode by itself, the Prussians will shoot it down. The wind is pushing it right over their lines!"

As I learned later from the caretaker's gossip, one of the balloonists was the famous young patriot, Leon Gambetta. He did not desert Paris as the caretaker's wife presumed, but rather he made his daring escape to organize the resistance and bring relief to the besieged city.

Instantly Gambetta became a hero to the citizens of Paris. His unusual method of transportation was used many more times during the fall and winter of that year, often bringing a bit of food and ammunition to the blockaded capital.

In spite of Gambetta and other patriotic Frenchmen's efforts, the news from the battlefields was bad. The only way of communication between Paris and the rest of the country was through carrier pigeons, since radio and telephones have not yet been invented. The pigeons were often shot by the enemy snipers and their messages intercepted. Occasionally, the pigeons were shot and eaten by the starving Parisians. The balloons were also unreliable: many exploded before taking to the air or were carried by wind directly into the enemy's hands. There were not enough balloonists who knew how to navigate the cumbersome conveyances.

I was proud to have had witnessed the first balloon flight. What a great adventure it must have been, I reflected. Too bad that such adventure was not possible for anyone of my ilk!

By January it became clear that the enemy's blockade of Paris was total. To add to the miseries of the besieged city, the Prussians began a bombardment of Paris. What did they want? I thought in anger. Didn't they get Alsace and Loraine? Didn't our government agree to pay them billions of franks as an indemnity?

One night I was awakened by the sound of a loud blast. The house trembled as the bay windows splintered into thousands of sharp fragments, covering the floor at my feet with a carpet of shattered glass. Were it not for the heavy velvet draperies, I would have been scarred and imbedded with shards. A stream of freezing winter air rushed into the room, clearing the stale odors of the past months. I became aware of smoke that drifted in through the shattered windows. A fire was burning somewhere near . . . I fervently hoped that our house would be spared.

I heard the shouts and screams of people as they rushed to put out the fire, and then, the deep, booming sounds of more explosions.

The enemy intensified its bombardment in preparation for an all-out attack on the city. With each new explosion my strings reverberated, echoing the tinkling of crystal chandeliers. When the first pale rays of winter sun broke through the torn draperies, I could see that the street below was littered with broken glass and shattered masonry. It was covered with a thick layer of red brick dust, as if blood had been spilled on the pavement.

The intense bombardment continued for three weeks, when finally, the city was forced to capitulate before the superior armies of Bismarck.

The people of Paris found it difficult to accept the sight of the triumphant Prussians making their entrance into the city. The citizens expressed their indignation over the surrender by staying inside their homes and ignoring the march of the arrogant conquerors along the Champs d'Élysée.

From the vantage point of the bay window I watched how column after column of Prussian Horse Guards trotted along the broad avenue, their banners unfurled, their marching bands playing. The men wore bronze spiked helmets that reflected the sun and shone like gold. The officers were attired in spotless white tunics with golden epaulettes and tight-fitting red or sky-blue britches, all encrusted with gold braid.

I had to admit that they were handsome people, those blond conquerors sitting high on their well-fed horses. They rode along the avenue expecting the Parisians to pay them homage as the victors, but the city looked dead. If they cared to look closer, they would have noticed many black flags of mourning draped around the lampposts. The balcony of our house, too, was draped with a black flag. The caretaker, an old patriot, made sure that his sentiments would be known to the conquerors.

The Prussians did not stay long in Paris. Our government must have paid them enough to leave the city.

Just as well, for a revolution broke out in Paris on the eighteenth of March 1871.

Oh, how I longed to know what was going on in the streets of Paris! As it was, all my information came to me from the caretaker or his wife, who held contrary opinions. I could hear the sounds of gunshots as the citizens fought, killing one another for the sake of an idea, which was different with each group. Some demanded a republic; the others wanted the Emperor to return from exile; still the others wished for a brand new King. "How silly these humans are!" I thought in exasperation. "They should take an example from the orchestras. We, the musical instruments are all different, yet we perform in harmony with one another. We complement each other, instead of fighting for dominance."

The culmination of the revolution, known in history as *the French Commune of 1871*, occurred in May. The troops of the National Assembly, which represented the provinces of France, entered the rebellious Paris. Through my bay window, I watched the events taking place with morbid fascination.

I saw dozens of armed men hurl furniture and bedding on the street below. They were building a barricade across the street, trying to stop the advancing troops of the National Assembly. Women tossed pillows and mattresses out of the upper story windows and the ever-present street urchins loosened stones from the pavements to be used as weapons against the forthcoming attack. The street was boiling with activity. Among the insurgents I recognized our caretaker. He was directing a group of husky young men in carting heavy furniture. I could not believe my eyes. They were taking it out of *our house*! Before I could imagine what would be the reaction of my master if he only knew what was happening to his priceless furnishings, three young men, led by our caretaker, burst into the salon.

"Take this sofa and that cabinet!" the caretaker commanded. He sported a red armband on his sleeve and his voice was full of authority. The young men lifted the heavy pieces effortlessly. They dragged them through the door and dropped them off the balcony to the street below. I heard a loud thud as the priceless wood frames of the sofa and the cabinet broke at impact. "How barbaric!" I thought, not ever suspecting that a similar fate was awaiting me.

"The piano will block at least half the street," suggested one of the young men.

"It will never clear the balcony," objected the caretaker.

"We can carry it through the front door," insisted the young man.

"All right. Let's try. It's very heavy, you'll need more help."

The young man stepped to the balcony. "Hey, Pierre, Luc, anybody, come over here. Give us a hand!" he shouted. Two more burly men in workmen's clothing appeared before me. Together they pushed me across the room and carried me down the marble staircase, through the front door, right to the street. I tried to resist their rough handling, but to no avail. There were four of them against one—me. I succeeded, however, in dropping my lid on the fingers of one of them, making him howl in pain. They pushed me toward a pile of furniture, broken horse carts and doors wrested out of their frames, and tried to turn me over on my side. They grabbed me by my keyboard and I cried in anguish, calling for help.

Miraculously help arrived, just when I was about to give up all hope. A young, pale man, no more than twenty, dressed poorly and wearing the red band of the Revolution, came running down the street. "Stop!" he yelled, "Don't break the piano! Stop at once!" The burly revolutionaries hesitated. There was authority in the stranger's voice as he fought his way through the crowd toward our group. He looked ill. His cheeks were ablaze with fever and he breathed in fast, short gasps, as if in pain. His dark, curly hair was moist and plastered against his perspiring forehead.

"This is a valuable musical instrument and not a heap of worthless wood," he was finally able to say between the gasps for air. "You are civilized men. Don't destroy beauty."

"Who are you? Are you the owner?" someone yelled.

"I wish I were the owner. I am just a poor musician."

"Then what's to you if it's broken or not? It's not yours."

"But don't you understand? It is an object of beauty. It is the *Pleyel!* Don't destroy it, I beg of you! Listen!" He tore open the lid over my keys and began to play the great patriotic song of France, the *"Marseillaise."*

"Allons enfants de la Patrie," he sang feverishly, his voice breaking with emotion. Surprised and moved by his fiery, eloquent performance, the mood of the crowd changed. The barricade builders joined the young musician in the rousing song until the whole street reverberated with their lusty voices. Gratefully, I gave my all to my rescuer. I knew that I would be spared.

"Who are you?" asked one of the older men. "What's your name?"

"Bernard Dubois. I am a musician. I live around the corner," the young man replied still caressing my keys with his long, thin fingers. "I am grateful to you for sparing this instrument. You'll never . . ." Bernard did not finish. A loud shot split the air and Bernard fell at my feet, wounded. There was another shot and a bullet grazed my side.

"To the barricade!" yelled the old man, assuming command. People rushed to the safety of the half-completed barricade. "Someone attend to the wounded!" ordered the commander as he, too, ran to the barricade, loading his rifle as he ran.

I saw a young girl step out of the crowd and kneel beside Bernard. She tore a piece of cloth from her petticoat and made a tourniquet from it, applying it to his leg. "I'll take you home, Monsieur. Can you walk?" she asked.

"I think so . . . But first, please help me find some cover for this piano. Look, the bullet made a hole in its side. Please, help me move it." He struggled to his feet and started to pull me toward the nearest building.

"Don't do it! Look, you're bleeding" the girl protested.

"Please, Mademoiselle!" Bernard pleaded, stubbornly trying to pull me out of danger.

"Oh, all right. Let me help you." She joined him and together they pulled me a few feet, but the pavement was rough, with many stones missing and my legs got stuck in the holes.

"Don't just stand there", the girl cried to a group of women who cowed near the wall. "Help us!" A couple of them broke away from the wall and came to our aid. Together they moved me under a tunnel-like entrance of a house.

"Thank you," whispered Bernard, leaning on the girl for support. His face was white from the loss of blood. "What's your name?"

"Jacqueline," the girl said shyly.

"Jacqueline," he repeated. "What a lovely name." His eyes clouded and he slid to the ground, unconscious.

How I wished that I could help him! He saved me from destruction, but all I could do was to stand there, big and clumsy, my side smarting from the bullet wound, and no one, not even Bernard realizing the depth of feeling within my heart.

"He's going to die if we don't get him to a doctor," a woman whispered to Jacqueline.

The girl stared at the bloodless face of the young musician. Her face hardened, "I won't let him die," she said. "I'll get him a doctor."

"Wait until the shooting stops," the woman said, but Jacqueline ignored her. She threw her shawl over her red hair and disappeared into the battle outside.

THREE

Jacqueline returned accompanied by an elderly man, who was dressed in an old-fashioned long coat and knee britches. The shooting outside had subsided and the women who had helped us, left. I watched as the doctor ripped the seam of Bernard's trouser leg and cleaned and bandaged his nasty wound. The young man remained unconscious.

"We must take him home. Do you know where he lives?" the doctor asked.

"No. He just said that he lived near-by." Jacqueline was holding the young man's head on her lap, wiping his pale, moist face with a handkerchief. The old doctor and the girl looked helplessly at one another.

"We can't leave him here . . . Where's everybody?" the doctor kept muttering under his breath as he shuffled outside the ornate gate to scan the deserted street. Through a crack in the open gate, I could see the barricade, a pathetic pile of broken furniture looming in the falling darkness. No long did it look menacing. It was hard to believe that only a few hours before it had been alive, bristling with dozens of armed men. Who had won the skirmish?

The doctor returned. A look of disillusionment spread over his round, owlish face. "No one's about! They all seemed to have vanished into the air. Not a soul to be found."

Bernard stirred and opened his eyes. He tried to sit up, but his strength was drained by the loss of blood. He fell back onto Jacqueline's lap.

"Don't move, young man. Just tell us, where do you live?" the doctor said kneeling at his side.

"Rue de la Cloche, around the corner . . . number ten . . . in the cellar . . ." He closed his eyes again.

The doctor stood up with an effort. "Well, my girl," he said gruffly, "we must take him to his home. How can we carry this fellow, is beyond me." He looked at the wounded man at his feet, not knowing what to do. "We can't pull him. It will kill him, for sure."

"I have an idea, Doctor," Jacqueline said shyly. "Perhaps we could *wheel* him on the top of the piano. You know, like on a wagon."

"Very good thinking, my girl!" The doctor laughed. His face, so serious before, dissolved into a web of kindly wrinkles. "Why, of course! The piano has *wheels*! All we have to do is to push!"

And that was exactly what they did. Somehow these two weaklings, an old man and a fragile girl of sixteen, lifted Bernard, placed him on my lid and pushed us out of the courtyard. Prudently they avoided the cobblestone street and wheeled me along the broad sidewalk without a mishap.

Once in front of Bernard's lodgings they stopped. The gates to the house were securely locked. "What next?" said the doctor acknowledging Jacqueline's leadership.

"We'll knock on the door and ask for help," the girl replied with a shrug. The doctor knocked on the tiny window cut in the large door with the word "*Concierge*" written above it.

Almost at once the little window was partially opened. The unfriendly face of the concierge, the building caretaker, peered at us with suspicion. "What do you want?" she demanded puffing on a fat cigar. Then, recognizing the motionless body of Bernard, she threw her cigar aside, not caring where it might fall, and flung the door open. "What have you done to him?" she screamed, rushing through the door in her carpet slippers. "You murdered him! You monsters!" She threw herself at the doctor with the savagery of a tigress.

"Wait, wait, Madame, we did not harm him," cried Jacqueline, flinging herself between them. "This is Doctor Morin and he helped Monsieur Dubois. He saved his life!"

The concierge hesitated. "Is it true?" she demanded of the good doctor.

"Yes, Madame, indeed it is true," the doctor said. "A sniper seriously wounded this young gentleman. This child, here," he pointed to the girl, "summoned me for help. I did what I could. Now, if you don't mind, please lead us to the young man's lodgings, so that we can make him comfortable."

The concierge calmed down. "This way," she said, placing her own considerable weight behind me and helping to push me onto the courtyard.

I saw a small double door leading into a basement flat. The concierge opened it with a rusty iron key and I saw a poor, grey room lacking furniture or rugs. "This way," the concierge repeated, helping Jacqueline and the doctor carry Bernard into the room. I was all but forgotten in the middle of the courtyard.

"Is he your son, Madame?" I heard Jacqueline asking the old woman.

"Oh, no, my child," she replied. "He is just a tenant. But I love him as if he were my son. He is a genius. He writes the most beautiful songs in the whole world! And he sings them to me." Her voice sounded tender, as if she were a different person, rather than a baleful old woman of a few minutes before.

The door was closed and I ceased to hear their conversation. "What will happen to me now?" I thought in anticipation of another disaster. "I can't stay here, exposed to the elements and the vandals . . ." As the time crept slowly by, my hope for a miraculous solution to my dilemma began to grow dimmer. It was completely dark now, except for a narrow slit of flickering candle light under Bernard's door. In spite of my worries about my future, I began to doze. Too much had happened to me during that day and I was fatigued. I was not prepared to deal with the vagaries of life. Having a philosophic bent, I decided to trust my lucky stars, an expression that I had learned from my former master, Monsieur Matignon.

The morning burst upon me with the chirping of birds and cooing of pigeons under the eaves of the building. The sunrays felt pleasant on my battered body, but I knew that the sun was my natural enemy. Were I to remain out of doors, the sun would crack my glossy finish, dry up my frame and lids and eventually destroy me.

With the coming of a new day my worry returned." What will become of me now that I am abandoned by everyone?" I thought. Although I was not far from the Matignon's mansion, I was sure that no one would bother to return me to my home. As I contemplated this hopeless predicament, I saw Jacqueline crossing the courtyard on her way to Bernard's flat. She carried a small pot covered with a towel. A strong aroma of onion soup filled the air. For a moment I forgot my troubles, overwhelmed by the feeling of envy. I had never tasted the savor of onion soup.

Jacqueline knocked on the door and the doctor opened it. He must have spent the night taking care of Bernard for he looked disheveled and tired.

"Ah, come in, come in, my child," he greeted the girl. "Our patient is much better this morning. He has been asking for you." He closed the door and I was left alone once more.

A pigeon landed on my lid and pecked at his reflection in my shiny, mirror-like finish. He walked sideways along the rim of my case, examining me with his nervous beady eyes.

"Shoo, shoo!" the concierge shouted from her window. "Get off Bertrand's piano!" The pigeon took off.

"Have I heard it right?" I thought with a start. "Did she say, '*Bernard's piano?*'" A happy premonition overwhelmed me. I knew it! Bernard would never abandon me!

The door to his flat was thrown open and doctor Morin appeared in its frame. "We might as well do it now," he said to Jacqueline who followed him. "Call the concierge to help us move this blasted piano inside."

Jacqueline ran across the yard and presently reappeared in the company of the concierge.

The three of them pushed and pulled. Somehow they managed to pull me through the door to Bernard's room, with only an inch to spare on each side.

Bernard anxiously watched our progress from his bed in the corner. His face was drawn and blanched but his eyes had a happy, feverish glow. My three friends left me standing in the center of the tiny room, for there was no other space for me.

"That was a capital idea, Madame Roget!" doctor Morin exclaimed, wiping his sweating brow with a checkered handkerchief. "Our young patriot saved this instrument from destruction, thus he deserves it!"

"But the owners . . . Who are they? Won't they demand that the piano be returned to them?" Bernard objected in a weak voice.

"Have no fear, *mon ami*," the concierge interrupted. "The owners, whoever they may be, will assume that the piano was destroyed along with the rest of their furniture." She puffed on her cigar again and I could not help but think how unfeminine she looked. But I did not allow my critical attitude toward the good lady to cloud my gratitude for my rescue. "Let her smoke her cigars," I thought. "As long as she doesn't leave them burning on my lid!"

"But it is *thievery*!" insisted Bernard.

"Don't worry, my boy," the doctor reassured him "When you get well, you can inquire in the neighborhood whose instrument it may be and return it to them. Meanwhile, you are doing them a good turn by keeping the piano out of harm's way. Your main duty now is not to worry but to get well. Do you understand?"

"Yes, Doctor," Bernard agreed meekly.

Bernard's recuperation was very slow, but his three dedicated friends never left his side. Madame Roget even gave up smoking her cigars when doctor Morin warned her that the smoke was harmful to their patient. As for Jacqueline, I could see that she was in love with the young musician. She was at his beck and call at all times, leaving his bedside only at night, when Madame Roget took over.

Bernard had me moved next to his bed. Although he was still too weak to play, he would touch my keys with one hand, smiling happily at the sonorous sounds that I produced. "As soon as I get well, I'll write a song for you," he said to Jacqueline, who looked at him with adoration.

Weeks passed. The rebels of the Paris Commune were defeated by the troops of the National Assembly and the civil war came to an end. As Bernard grew stronger and began to spend some time at my keyboard, I lost interest in the political situation. I became fascinated with my new young master. Bernard was a man of huge talent. I worked with him creating chords and arpeggios, harmonies, and tempos. I followed the conception of a musical theme from a few notes, played with a couple of fingers, until a complete composition would materialize as if out of nowhere. Bernard would play it for his friends, who showered him with compliments, but only I would know how much effort and energy it had cost him to write it down.

The song that he had promised to Jacqueline, with lyrics by Paul Verlaine, was a touching declaration of love. I was delighted. Neither doctor Marin nor the concierge had any idea of the blossoming love affair. The young people were discrete in the company of their elderly friends. But with me, they had no need for secrecy. I witnessed their first kiss and heard their plans for their future.

Bernard's health continued to improve. Doctor Morin recommended that he should start taking walks in the park, while Madame Roget cleaned his room.

One day, while the lovers were walking in the park, the old doctor knocked on our door.

"Come right in," cried Madame Roget who was dusting the room. "Bernard is in the park with Jacqueline."

"That's good," the doctor said, settling on the only chair in the room. "I wanted to talk to you privately, Madame. You realize, don't you, that our young man is very ill? Yes, he has an advanced case of consumption, that dreadful disease of the lungs, which we, physicians, call *tuberculosis.*"

"But he's feeling so much better now," objected the concierge. "He plays his piano, he writes his music . . ."

"Yes, he has recovered from his wounds, but it has nothing to do with his *main* illness. I am sorry, Madame, but our protégé is a doomed young man," he concluded sadly.

The concierge began to polish me furiously, smudging me with her tears that kept rolling silently down her withered cheeks. "What can we do to save him?" she finally sobbed. Before doctor Morin could answer, the young couple entered the room.

"Doctor Morin, Madame Roget, I am so glad that you're here!" Bernard cried. "Jacqueline and I decided to be get married!" His face was radiant. His arm was draped around Jacqueline's shoulders and the girl blushed, looking prettier than ever. "You are the first to know!"

"They are *not* the first to know!" I wanted to cry. "*I am* the first to know!" But of course I remained silent. This was one of many times in my life when I regretted not being born a human being.

"Why, this is the best news I have heard in a long time!" exclaimed Madame Roget dropping her dust cloth and rushing to embrace the young couple. Doctor Morin, forgetting the aches and pains of the old age, did a sprightly jig, delighted with the good news.

The wedding took place a few days later. Jacqueline and Bernard were both orphans, thus there was no need for parental consent and a prolonged engagement. Doctor Morin and Madame Roget accompanied the young couple to the City Hall to act as witnesses.

When the little wedding party returned home, they were greeted by the sounds of a wedding march. Bernard's best friend played it, with my help, needless to say.

"Camille Saint-Saëns!" the bridegroom cried in surprise. "How did you know about my marriage?"

I could hardly believe my ears. The man who played the Mendelssohn's famous wedding march was Saint-Saëns! The great composer and one of the most famous organists in the world! He was touching my keys! What honor! What rapture!

Camille Saint-Saëns smiled. "News travels fast among the musicians," he said. "I've also heard about your exploits on the barricades. What foolishness! You were lucky that you were wounded in the legs. Were it your hands you would have been forced to bid *adieu* to your career!" He was smiling, but I knew that he meant his words to be taken seriously.

"Oh, Monsieur Saint-Saëns," gushed doctor Morin, "I've been your admirer for years! Every Sunday I go to the church of St. Madeleine just to hear you play. Allow me to shake your hand!" Embarrassed by such unadulterated praise, Saint-Saëns extended his hand to the doctor. "I am delighted that you like my playing. An artist is always ready to be praised. Praise is our sustenance. But introduce me to your charming bride, Bernard," Saint-Saëns said changing the subject.

"Oh, I am so sorry, Camille, I am so absentminded . . ." awkwardly Bernard introduced Jacqueline to his friend.

The concierge beamed at the newlyweds. She seemed to know Saint-Saëns quite well. I suspected that it was she, who had arranged his appearance in our modest lodgings.

Saint-Saëns brought with him a huge basket full of delicacies and a bottle of champagne. The concierge spread a tablecloth over my top and the wedding party used me as an improvised table. I felt smothered under the cloth, but decided to be a good sport and suffer in silence. After all, it was Bernard's wedding!

Saint-Saëns came to visit us almost daily. I was fascinated with his appearance. He was not handsome. He was stocky and rather short. He had a high and somewhat bumpy brow and his hair was cut very short, contrary to the current fashion. He wore a small beard and a bristling moustache that did not hide the deep lines that seemed to start at his nostrils and ran to the corners of his mouth. His nose resembled a bird's beak and his eyes were a little prominent, as if he had trouble with his thyroid.

Saint-Saëns was a prolific composer. Like Mozart, he was a child prodigy, appearing at the age of four and a half as a pianist in a performance of a Beethoven sonata for violin and piano. At the age of eleven, he played concertos by Mozart and Beethoven at *La Salle Pleyel*, my own Alma Mater. He was only eighteen when his *Symphony # 1* was performed in Paris to a great acclaim. Success and adulation followed.

I have learned these fascinating details by listening to the conversations between doctor Marin, who was the composer's admirer and Bernard, who was his protégé. I was in "seventh heaven," as they say, when Saint-Saëns would sit at my keyboard and play some pieces from his work-in-progress. Many, many years later, when radio was invented, I heard the same melodies over the airwaves. It made me proud to realize that perhaps I was the only one in the world, who had heard this very music during its conception. Thus, I have heard snatches of his great opera *"Samson and Delilah"* long before it was written. I also heard the celebrated *"Dance Macabre,"* while it was still in a sketchy form and which eventually became one of the favorite short pieces written for the orchestra. But I am getting ahead of my story.

Saint-Saëns knew that my young master was very ill and he tried to help. I saw him giving money to the concierge to pay for Bernard's rent and board. He attempted to pay doctor Morin for his services also, but the old gentleman proudly refused. "Bernard is my friend. I don't charge my friends for my ministrations," he announced huffily.

As another winter approached, Bernard's health took a turn for the worse. He coughed incessantly and I saw Jacqueline cry covertly, for she must have guessed the truth about her husband's condition. Soon he started spitting blood. He spent most of his days half-sitting in bed, propped high upon several pillows. His frail body was constantly shaken by long paroxysms of coughing that left him exhausted and limp. He was too weak to compose.

At the beginning of January Saint-Saëns came to bid us good-bye. He was leaving on one of his many concert tours. As usual he brought with him a basketful of provisions and wine.

"I would like you to hear a new composition of mine," he said to Bernard. "It is called '*Le Rouet d'Omphale*.' It is a *symphonic* poem, but I like it also as a *piano* piece. I took the idea from Franz Liszt's tone poems," he smiled shyly, as if apologizing that he was not the originator of the new form.

"Who is Omphale?" Jacqueline asked the very question that intrigued me.

"My dear child, my composition '*Le Rouet d'Omphale* is a story from Greek mythology. Fulfilling the decree of the Olympian gods, the great hero Heracles was ordered to serve queen Omphale for several years at her spinning wheel and wear women's clothing."

"Poor Heracles! How humiliating for such a hero!" Jacqueline smiled.

"Don't worry your pretty head, my dear. It's only an ancient myth, a fairytale. Besides, Heracles didn't suffer much. The beautiful Omphale fell in love with him and took him as a lover. He wore the women's clothes only when he was *working* at her spinning wheel!"

Everyone laughed as Saint-Saëns seated himself in front of my keyboard and began to play. Fast, fluid music rippled through my strings, filling the dingy room with glorious sounds. There was something hypnotic in the melody that made me want to continue to play, and play as if I were spinning music.

Saint-Saëns finished his short piece with a flourish and turned to his audience. "What do you think of it?"

"Marvelous! Simply marvelous!" my master cried with enthusiasm. "I predict that '*The Spinning Wheel*' will become a favorite of concert audiences!"

How right he was! Even now, more than a hundred years later, one can still hear '*Omphale's Spinning Wheel*' played by symphony orchestras and piano virtuosi throughout the world.

Camille Saint-Saëns left. A deep melancholy surrounded our small group again, as Bernard's health continued to deteriorate. Doctor Morin, a widower, practically moved in with the young couple, often sleeping in a chair near his patient. As the weeks passed, hope for Bernard's recovery dimmed progressively. Then, one windy morning, when a monotonous cold rain lashed against our ground-level windows, Bernard quietly expired. Jacqueline was sleeping on the cot at the foot of his bed and doctor Marin was dozing in his chair, so I was the only one who was aware of Bernard's death. My extra-sensitive perception of sound alerted me that Bernard's breathing had stopped. My young master was gone.

When Jacqueline and the doctor awoke and realized that Bernard was dead, they both broke down in torrents of tears. Presently, the concierge arrived with a bowl of porridge for Bernard, but one look at the peaceful face of the young musician and the weeping wife and doctor Morin at his bedside told her what had happened. She made the sign of the cross and knelt at his bedside. "I loved him as if he were my son," she sobbed. Then, making an effort to regain control over her sorrow, she rose to her feet to make the arrangements for the funeral.

A few hours later, the undertakers brought in a wooden coffin. They covered me with a black cloth and lifted the heavy coffin on the top of my lid. Once again I was to bear my master's body.

Several of Bernard's friends came to bid him *adieu*. They carried his remains to a catafalque drawn by two black horses with black plumes on their heads. Through the window I watched the sad little procession leave the courtyard. Silently, I too, said good-bye to my master, who had left the world much too soon to fulfill the promise of his talent.

"What will become of me?" I thought. Maybe it was selfish to think of myself at that moment, but what, indeed, could be the future of someone, who had no power over his own destiny?

FOUR

The days following Bernard's death were the saddest of my life. Doctor Morin insisted that Jacqueline move in with Madame Roget. I was abandoned and forgotten in the cold room. A heavy padlock was attached to the door and when I heard it snap, I lost all touch with the outside world. At first I thought it would be only a day or two before Jacqueline would return to our unhappy room. But the days chased one another into weeks and still no one came to the empty lodgings. Soon I lost count of time and succumbed to the stupor of loneliness and despair. My strings loosened and then tightened in the freezing air of the empty basement and if someone were to strike a chord, I would have responded with a tinny, false sound.

Nevertheless, deep in my heart, I still hoped for a happy solution. I hoped that Camille Saint-Saëns would return and claim me for himself.

Then, one day the padlock was finally removed. Jacqueline stood on the threshold, hesitating to enter the room. Her sorrow had matured her and removed the glow of youth from her cheeks. "Hurry, *mon ange*, collect anything that you want to keep. We'll sell the rest to a junk dealer." Madame Roget squeezed her formidable bulk past Jacqueline. She opened the shutters and the bright light of spring burst into the damp basement.

"A junk dealer! Is that what is going to be my fate?" I thought in horror. I watched Jacqueline gather a few possessions. When she had finished packing, she paused, slowly scanned the room and bid it good-bye.

"Don't be so sad, my dear," Madame Roget said embracing the girl. "You're young and someday you'll love again. I am glad that doctor Morin will teach you the art of nursing. It is a fine, noble profession and you'll be able to support yourself for the rest of your life, or until you marry someone!"

The girl smiled through her tears. "I will be fine, Madame Roget, but I'll never love anyone as much as I loved my Bernard!" They left, without locking the door.

"If only the Matignon family knew that I am just a few blocks away!" I thought desperately hoping for another miracle. But this time there was no young eager musician, or anyone to come to my aid.

I heard the snorting of a horse and the creaking of a rickety wagon in our courtyard. Presently, the concierge entered the room in the company of a bearded man dressed in a long, threadbare black coat that reached to his ankles. He wore a flat round hat with a wide brim and a heavy gold chain crossed his chest from one side pocket to another. He ran his fingers expertly over my keys and then lifted my lid, examining my strings. He tested the pedals and bent under my belly to look if everything was in place. I was surprised that such an odd-looking character seemed to know exactly what to look for in a piano.

"I'll take it," he said to Madame Roget. "But I won't pay what you're asking. It is badly damaged. Do you see those holes?" He pointed to the chipped wood where I was grazed by a bullet on the barricade. "It will cost a fortune to repair."

"All right, all right, give me anything," she interrupted, obviously interested in making the sale. I suspected that the concierge thought that any amount of money would be a profit since I did not cost anything to acquire. She wanted to get rid of me, lest someone may start asking embarrassing questions. Whichever her reasons, she did not haggle over my sale.

The dealer walked around me once more. "This piano comes from a famous factory," he said. "I won't ask you how you got it, on condition that you don't tell anyone to whom you have sold it. Agreed?"

"Agreed. What about the other furniture? The bed? What will you give me for it?"

"Nothing. I don't want it." The dealer took a large shabby purse out of his pocket. He counted out several coins into Mme Roget's outstretched hand and shouted through the open door for his helper.

A young man appeared, dressed like the dealer, a copy of the old man. Together they expertly removed my legs, turned me on my side and pushed me onto a wagon, using a ramp covered with padding. Obviously they knew how to transport a piano. I wasn't their first one.

A new optimism lifted my spirits. "They must be professional piano dealers," I thought observing that their wagon was also padded to protect the instruments from nicks and chips. "Maybe they have a Salon, like Monsieur Duval."

I hoped for a glimpse of Jacqueline or doctor Morin before I left them forever, but they were nowhere to be seen. Even Madame Roget did not bother to see me off. She was busy cleaning the basement flat for its next occupant.

"Just as well," I thought. "Apparently my life is destined to be a conglomeration of chance encounters."

The piano dealer and his son covered me with a quilted blanket and secured me to the sides of the wagon with stout ropes. They climbed on the driver's seat, turning their attention to the horse. With one mighty pull, the animal started the wagon moving. One more episode of my life was over and another one, still unknown to me, was about to begin.

The piano dealer took great care of me. Cautiously he and his son sandpapered my scratches, and then filled them with a wood-sealing compound. They polished the repairs until only the most practiced eye would have noticed that I had ever been injured. Then, they invited a piano tuner who worked on me for three solid days loosening or tightening my strings, whichever was indicated, placing his ear close to my vibrating strings, until I was tuned to perfection.

The old dealer walked around me, rubbing his hands with joy. "What a piano! What a great instrument!" he kept murmuring, playing a few rippling arpeggios. I could see that he was a musician and he fully appreciated me.

When I was polished and dusted once more, the dealers moved me into a large room that was crowded with pianos of all makes. It was a far cry from the elegant Salon Duval, where only three or four instruments were on display. In this place, there must have been twenty or more pianos, standing shoulder to shoulder, like soldiers on parade, all grinning with their shiny teeth, eager to make the best impression. I felt discouraged. "What chance has one to be noticed among so many competitors?" I thought.

But my luck still held, although at the time I did not consider myself to be lucky. Within a week an elegant lady bought me for her ten-year-old nephew.

"A child is going to bang on my keys!" I thought in despair. I could already anticipate the pain I would suffer. I saw such a child just a few days before in the dealer's show room. The little monster attacked one piano after another, not bothering to use his fingers, but rather his fists, his elbows, and his knuckles. He would have used his feet also, if he only could figure out how to do it! All the pianos in the dealer's showroom groaned and cried under his rough treatment, all of us hoping that we would be spared the dubious privilege of being chosen. As it turned out, our dealer's prices were too high for the family and so none of us was subjected to the years of abuse.

No wonder then, when I heard that the lady was buying me for her young nephew, I was full of apprehension.

Fortunately my fears were groundless. From the moment I was delivered to a small apartment of Monsieur Debussy and met his son, Achille-Claude, I knew that I would be in good hands. As the boy began to play, crisp harmonies of a Bach fugue filled the room. I was singing with joy. *The boy was a prodigy!*

At the age of ten he was playing like a real professional. The boy was too short, so his aunt placed two thick volumes of Beethoven sonatas on the piano stool to raise him to the correct height.

The aunt applauded. "It was wonderful!" she exclaimed. "I am sure, Madame de Fleurville will be pleased at last! She's such a demanding teacher. She kept complaining that Achille-Claude's talents *demanded* the best possible instrument. Now-he has it. The *Pleyel*, no less!" She kissed the boy, as his mother beamed with pride. His father seemed to be bewildered by the ladies' enthusiasm. I suspected that he did not have an ear for music and could not fully appreciate me.

However, I was overjoyed. To be recognized as *"the best possible instrument"* was a proper evaluation, I thought immodestly. I was looking forward to helping this young prodigy to develop into a mature talent. It appealed to my imagination and flattered my vanity.

Next day I met Madame de Fleurville, the boy's teacher. She was a severe-looking woman, who dressed in dark, outmoded clothes, wore her hair in a knot at the base of her head, contrary to the elaborate hair fashions of Parisian ladies.

Seated at the piano, she looked suddenly transformed. A soft, dreamy expression lighted her face as she closed her eyes and ran her fingers over my keys. Madame de Fleurville used to be a pupil of Chopin. He was her hero, her god, and her inspiration.

She had only a few students, but each of them was a choice pupil. Her most promising student was my new master, Achille-Claude. She spent long hours with him, well beyond her usual lesson, playing Chopin and Liszt for him, explaining the intricacies and differences in their styles. Listening to Madame de Fleurville talk about music, proved to be very educational for me, as well. I learned a lot about Chopin and his *grande passion,* the famous writer Amandine Aurore Dupin, whose *nom de plume* was Georges Sand. Many of Chopin's best-known pieces were dedicated to her.

Madame de Fleurville disliked Georges Sand. She blamed the volatile writer for Chopin's untimely death at the age of only thirty-nine. She described to us Chopin's funeral service in the famous Madeleine Church, where Mozart's *Requiem* was performed in Chopin's memory. With tears rolling down her cheeks, she told us that a small urn of Polish earth that her hero had cherished ever since he had left his native country, was placed into his coffin.

Madame Roustan, the dotting aunt who bought me for Achille-Claude, was often present during those long sessions, sitting quietly in the corner of the small drawing room, knitting a shawl for the teacher or a scarf for her nephew. She was always dressed in the latest fashion and I presumed that she was rich. It was an anachronism to observe her *knitting*, as if she were an old lady of meager means. During the nine years that I had spent in the Debussy's household, the young Achille-Claude and his teacher must have acquired dozens of woolen scarves and shawls, all looking like one another.

I liked the Debussy family even though they were rather strange. The father was a taciturn man, who once had been wealthy, but had lost his money and was forced to engage in a variety of minor jobs. Mother had an explosive temperament. I saw her striking the young Achille-Claude across the face, only to be kissing him the next moment. The other four children lived with Madame Roustan and visited their parents only on Sundays. Maybe because the family was divided, the mother concentrated all her love and all her anger on Achille-Claude. She instinctively knew the boy was a genius and she singled him out for the lion's share of her emotions.

The apartment of the Debussy family was small and crowded with furniture, but I did not mind it. After living in the dark, damp basement of my late master, this place looked like a mansion to me.

Achille-Claude treated me with affection. He often played strange, haunting chords or dissonant-sounding passages, so different from Mozart or Beethoven or more contemporary composers, such as Chopin, Liszt or even my friend Saint-Saëns. He would sit on his two volumes of Beethoven sonatas, his eyes shut, his fingers barely touching my keys, improvising unusual, beautiful melodies. I felt a tingle of excitement as I responded to his touch, giving forth these new harmonies. I did not know it then, but I was witnessing the first timid steps of a new movement in music, which later became known to the world as *Impressionism*.

Achille-Claude was only eleven when he was accepted as a regular student at the Paris Conservatory. I still remember the jubilation at the little flat when the official letter of acceptance had arrived. Even the grouchy father was impressed." Well, I guess there is nothing that I can say to prevent my son from becoming a musician" he had to admit. "Somehow, I always hoped that he would become a sailor, a merchant mariner. At least, he would always have a job!"

"A sailor!" Madame de Fleurville cried in righteous indignation." Monsieur, you do not seem to realize that your son is going to be an *immortal!*"

"There, there," Madame Roustan patted the teacher's shoulder. "Don't get excited, my dear. We will watch with pride our Achille-Claude's progress. As for being *a sailor*", she looked at the boy's father and winked, "I am sure that our boy could become a sailor! Someday, he'll own a yacht of his own. He'll sail to the Côte d'Azur, in the company of some lovely lady. Our Achille-Claude is going to be famous and rich someday!"

"I don't care about his fame," the father insisted stubbornly, "But I would like him to be *rich.*" Everyone, including Madame de Fleurville, laughed. Madame Debussy frowned at her husband's rudeness, but instead of making a scene, invited the company to the table to celebrate Achille-Claude's good fortune.

After just a few days at the Conservatory, Achille-Claude decided to drop his first name. "My teacher told me the story of Achille, who is known in Greek mythology as Achilles. He was a great hero. He was made immortal when his mother dipped him into the waters of the sacred river Styx when he was an infant. No man, no sword, or arrow, or javelin could kill him. But there was one spot that made him vulnerable. The magic water did not touch the heel of his foot by which his mother held him when she dipped him into the Styx. Achilles was killed in the Trojan War by an arrow that penetrated his heel. I don't want to bear that name and be vulnerable in such a picayune way! I want to be known as Claude Debussy!"

The Conservatory teachers were pleased with his progress. Claude was a diligent student. Quite early he decided that his main interest, and talent, lay in composition, rather than virtuoso performance. He plunged into the study of harmony and orchestration. By the time he was fourteen, he had produced several songs for voice and piano to texts by Paul Verlaine, a famous poet, and the son-in-law of Madame de Fleurville. There was jubilation in the Debussy household when Claude had won several prizes for his compositions.

As he grew older, his music became more unorthodox. He complained to his aunt and Madame de Fleurville that his professors disapproved of his music. "They say that I write discordant music. Why can't I write what I *feel?* Why can't they listen to my music without knowing the *names* of the chords? They say that my chords don't exist! But they do exist! They are right there, within my head and within the piano!"

Claude continued to compose his music the way he felt it. He and I worked together, deep into the night, enchanted and inflamed with the new tonalities and combinations of sound that had not been heard before. I was as excited about his new harmonies as he was, for I could clearly see the possibilities of coexistence of baroque, romantic and impressionistic music living in harmony.

Eventually, some of his professors came to the same conclusion. Even though they disapproved his rebellious innovations, they fell under the spell of his musical genius.

But, I am ahead of my story. By the time Claude was seventeen, he became a master of piano accompaniment. He could read any score and play it flawlessly. This ability impressed his teachers. One of his famous professors, Monsieur Marmontel, suggested that he should become the household pianist for a wealthy Russian lady, Madame von Meck, who was visiting France.

Claude was excited about the offer. The pay was high and he was to spend the summer in a graceful chateau on the Loire River and possibly, even travel abroad. I was sad to see him go, but also glad for this chance for him to get out into the world. I knew more than anyone, even more than his devoted aunt and Madame de Fleurville, how hard Claude worked during the past several years. He deserved that opportunity, even though it meant that I would be neglected.

Claude regularly wrote to his family about his travels with Madame von Meck's entourage through France, Switzerland and Italy. His mother read his letters every Sunday to the entire family, and again to Madame de Fleurville whenever she would come for a visit.

Claude enjoyed his duties. He described the von Meck's family as cultured and charming. "They all speak French without a trace of a Russian accent" he wrote in one letter. "They are *arrogantly rich*," he noted in another.

I waited with impatience for Claude's return. The family went to the railroad station to meet him as I stood, newly polished and tuned, waiting for him in the tiny drawing room. I heard the rubber wheels of a carriage and I knew immediately that Claude had arrived. He entered the apartment looking tanned and healthy, wearing fashionable clothes and a green tie, his favorite color. He even sported a small new moustache that made him look debonair, beyond his seventeen years. His voice had also changed. It had lost its boyish resonance and acquired the deeper tones of a grown man.

He rushed to me and struck several dissonant chords resolving them in traditional chords. "It's good to be home!" he cried happily. I couldn't agree more.

Claude resumed his studies at the Conservatory and before long, another year had passed. As summer approached he wrote to Madame von Meck asking whether she would like to have him work for her again. He waited impatiently for her reply.

At last he received the long-awaited letter. The lady was happy to have him spend three or four months with her family on one of her estates in Russia. She offered him a considerable increase in salary plus all expenses. She also asked him for a favor. She wanted a *French piano*. Perhaps Erard or Pleyel. Since she did not send any money for the purchase, and he obviously lacked funds to do it on his own, Claude presumed that she wanted him to bring along his *own* French piano. After all, it was a *Pleyel.* The family discussed the situation and it was decided that I would accompany Claude to Russia. I was beside myself with happiness.

A railroad agent was called for consultation and soon I was encased in a specially built padded crate and loaded into a baggage car bound for Moscow, Russia. My young master rode in a second-class compartment, his luggage bulging with music paper. We both looked forward to our summer in Russia, the land of Tchaikovsky and samovars, ballet and caviar, the Russia of mystery and magnificent music, the Russia of people, who like the Italians, were born to sing. Russia, an enigma of a country.

FIVE

We arrived in Moscow in the afternoon. As the train pulled slowly under the glass-domed railroad terminal, I began to feel the familiar excitement of anticipation. What new adventures lay ahead of me in this strange land, whose language I did not understand?

Madame von Meck's secretary met us at the station. He was surprised that Debussy brought his own piano, but as any well-trained employee, he did not question the guest. Instead, he invited Debussy to be seated in a small carriage, while I would follow in an open peasant cart.

I felt nervous as I watched Claude and the secretary leave. I hoped that nothing adverse would happen to me and that I wouldn't get lost somewhere along the way. Crowds of strange-looking men and women surrounded me. They were dressed in dark, homespun, rough clothing, so different from the attire of the people in my native Paris. I realized that they were probably poor peasants, but even the poorest people in France wore shoes. These people were shod in webbed tree-bark contraptions tied to their feet with narrow leather cords over the strips of dirty buntings, like puttees. Most men wore heavy unkempt beards while women hid their hair under bright scarves. But they were friendly. When it became obvious that I was too heavy to lift, the peasants eagerly came to the aid of two baggage attendants. They lifted me onto the top of a cart filled with straw and tied ropes about me so I wouldn't fall off the cart. All the time they talked in a strange musical language, not a word of which sounded familiar to me.

Our progress through the streets of Moscow was very slow but I did not mind. The weather was warm and I was fascinated with the many contrasts of the city. There were wide, shady boulevards, like in Paris, studded with monuments and statuary, lined with handsome mansions behind ornate iron gates, yet, next to them, I could see ramshackle log houses and long stretches of grey, weather-beaten fences. The streets were crowded with handsome carriages, but next to them moved dirty carts, stuffed with rotten straw, just like the one I was riding in. We passed one street after another, until we came to an enormous red brick fortress studded with tall towers at regular intervals.

I presumed that it must be the famous Kremlin, the picture of which I had seen in one of Claude's books. It was an ancient rampart and its crenellated walls resembled hundreds of bristling letters **M**. Behind the walls I glimpsed at many churches with tall belfries topped by onion-shaped cupolas of glittering gold or brilliant blue. At the foot of the wall there was a park blazing with flowerbeds and paths sprinkled with yellow sand. People promenaded in the park, just like in the Jardin de Luxembourg in Paris, ladies hiding from the sun under white parasols and gentlemen sporting light-colored top hats. There were scarcely any poorly dressed people in the park. I presumed that it was the aristocratic part of the city.

As we turned the corner, still following the great wall of the fortress, which seemed to continue indefinitely, we came upon a huge open square. A fantastic church appeared before me. I had never imagined that such an intricate, fairytale-like structure had ever existed. The church had *nine* towers, varying in height, each topped with differently shaped multi-colored cupola. It was like a vision in a dream.

When Madame von Meck saw me being unloaded from the cart, she raised her eyebrow. "Don't you find, Monsieur Debussy, that it is rather extravagant for a young man of your modest means, to travel with his own instrument? We have plenty of pianos in Russia," she said icily.

Debussy blushed painfully. "You mentioned, Madame, that you wished to have a French piano and that you would pay for all expenses," he stuttered in embarrassment.

"What I meant was that I wished *to buy* a French piano," she emphasized. "I wanted you to *choose* a piano for me, which was all that I wanted. Ah, well. Take this instrument to the Green Salon," she told her secretary who followed her with a notepad writing down her orders.

"How was your trip?" she asked Claude. "Did you enjoy the sights of Moscow on the way to my house?"

"Oh, yes, Madame," Claude stuttered, still smarting after being humiliated.

As I was to learn later, when I heard Debussy describe to Madame his admiration of the fortress and the ancient church, the red brick fortress was indeed, the Kremlin and the church was the famous Cathedral of St. Basil the Blessed.

Madame von Meck told Claude that the Kremlin was originally built of wood, but was rebuilt after Napoleon's ill-fated invasion of Russia in 1812. Russians burned their own city rather than surrender to the French. "We've taught you a lesson," she said shaking her finger.

My young master did not like her sarcastic reference to the shameful pages of our history. Napoleon's invasion of Russia was still a painful collective memory for the French, but he swallowed his pride and asked the lady to tell him about the Cathedral.

"Oh, that is quite an interesting story," she said, graciously. "The Cathedral of St. Basil, the Blessed, had survived Napoleon's invasion. It was built by our Tsar, Ivan the Terrible. You probably have heard about him. He lived in the sixteenth century and as his name implies, he was very cruel. But, he also was the one who had defeated the Mongols and ended more than two hundred years of their domination of Russia. You undoubtedly read about it at school."

"Yes," Claude said, blushing. I knew that he was self-conscious about his lack of formal education; since he had entered the Conservatory of Music at eleven, his education was concentrated on studying music. It left practically no time for other subjects. He probably had never heard about the Mongol invasion. I certainly haven't heard about it.

"Tell me more," he begged.

"Well, to commemorate his victory over the Mongols, Tsar Ivan had ordered to build the Cathedral of St. Basil the Blessed. Six years later, when the Cathedral was finished, the legend goes, Tsar Ivan called the master builder to appear before him. 'I like the church that you've built,' he had said, rewarding the builder handsomely. 'Can you build another church as beautiful as this one?' 'Surely, Your Majesty,' answered the man, flattered by the Tsar's praise. 'I can build an even more beautiful one!' 'In that case, out with your eyes!' the Tsar cried. 'I want no one to have a church more beautiful than this one!' So, the builder was blinded," Madame von Meck concluded.

Debussy shuddered, thinking undoubtedly about this strange land and its cruel history.

The von Meck house reminded me of Paris. It stood behind a tall ornate iron fence, its colonnaded portico jutting into the cobble-stoned yard. The house was full of fine furniture and priceless objects d'art, much more plentiful and magnificent than those of the Matignon's. To me, who had tasted the luxury of the Matignon household, the atmosphere of the von Meck's mansion was familiar. But the young Debussy, who was used to the modest flat of his parents, felt intimidated by the riches of his Russian patroness.

Madame Nadezhda von Meck was the widow of a railroad magnate and the mother of nine or eleven children. I was never sure about their number. She adored music. She engaged my young master not only as a music teacher for her children, but also as an accompanist for herself and one of her daughters, who loved to sing. Beside these duties, Claude was also to be a member of her small chamber orchestra that played at her regular soirées.

Our patroness was a dark-haired, tall woman with a sallow complexion. She had close-set dark eyes and a long nose, with sharply defined narrow nostrils that made her look as if she constantly smelled something unpleasant. She might have been exotically attractive, when she was young, however at the time of our acquaintance, she was sinewy, and her hair was beginning to turn gray. Her thin, nervous fingers were always covered with several sparkling rings. Whenever she played piano (and she was a good pianist), she took her rings off. She complained that they made her hands feel too heavy for Chopin's nocturnes or Mozart minuets. The rings remained on the music stand above my keyboard, sometimes for days, which gave me plenty of time to admire them. The maids, who dusted me daily, often tried the rings on their own fingers furtively glancing at the door. They undoubtedly were tempted to hide them in their pockets, but they never tried. They would quickly replace the rings on the stand at the first sound of the footsteps. "Madame would never miss her rings," I thought. "Each day she wears different ones."

The Green Salon was one of several in the great sixty-three room mansion. I have not seen the private quarters of the family, but I did admire the salons and libraries and game rooms on the main floor. The rooms led one into another, connected by ornate double French doors. Through the open doors I could see the enfilades of richly furnished rooms in both directions, each equipped with a piano, or a harp, or even an organ. The walls of the rooms were covered with paintings in heavy gold frames or with bright mirrors. The floors, made of intricately inlaid parquet, were partially hidden by enormous Aubusson carpets, or thick Persian rugs.

"How can one live in such a place?" I thought in awe. "It's a palace, not a family home!"

But a family home it was and soon I was to make my acquaintance with its numerous occupants. Not all of Madame's children lived at home. Two or three of them were already married, but those who still remained with her were a lively group.

In addition to the children, there were French, English and German governesses, several male tutors in all subjects of elementary and secondary education, male and female dancing teachers, singing teachers, equestrian instructors, nurses and two musicians, in addition to Claude. There were butlers and maids, cooks and coachmen, gardeners and footmen. There were laundresses and seamstresses, valets and doormen. All these multitudes of people were in constant movement throughout the house during the day, but at night, they would become invisible, except for the musicians and one or two of older children, and of course, the male servants, such as butlers and footmen. At night, the house would be filled with guests assembled in the Grand Salon. From my smaller Green Salon I could clearly see the largest part of the Grand Salon. The other part was reflected in the mirror, thus I felt as if I were in the Grand Salon myself, among the privileged guests.

Madame herself would play the piano, a huge concert grand German *Bechstein*. I felt that I was just as good, if not better than that German behemoth, but I was powerless to prove it.

Sometimes, Madame played with Claude, in four hands, but more often she sat in her high throne-like chair, listening pensively to her household Chamber Orchestra.

One night at the end of the program of chamber music Madame sighed. "It was wonderful, but I wish I had an opera company of my own. Like King Ludwig of Bavaria. But alas, I can afford only a small chamber group!" I knew that she loved opera. She encouraged her daughters in their singing lessons and sometimes she, herself, would sing some haunting Russian songs written by Tchaikovsky especially for her. I loved those songs, so delicate and melancholy.

Among the children, who took instruction from Claude, I especially liked Sonya, a girl of fifteen. She had a lovely voice. Claude often accompanied her and I enjoyed blending my voice with hers. She was tall for her age and already looked elegant with her long golden hair cascading freely down her back. She was a pretty girl and obviously her mother's favorite. I often saw her curled up in the great chair in the library, with a book on her lap. She read voraciously, mostly the French novels of Alexandre Dumas. Her mother encouraged Sonya to read, placing no restrictions on her choice of books. One day Sonya appeared for her singing lesson with camellias in her hair. "I have just finished La *Dame Aux Camelias*, she announced dramatically to her singing teacher. "I loved that book. I know that Verdi wrote his opera *La Traviata* based on that novel. I want to learn Violetta's arias from *La Traviata.*"

I was delighted by her announcement. It gave me an opportunity to learn more of Verdi's music. As the result, I became the lover and connoisseur of Verdi, thanks to the lovely Russian girl in Moscow.

Although I enjoyed working with Sonya, helping her in developing her coloratura soprano, I was really intrigued by her mother. Listening to the conversations of the members of the family and overhearing the gossip of the guests, I learned about the strange relationship between my hostess and the composer Peter Tchaikovsky. Luckily for me, the members of Russian higher society spoke French among themselves. They reverted to their native Russian only while addressing the servants. They spoke French even to their domestic animals and riding horses. Their snobbery made it easy for me to understand their conversations, although eventually, after many years, I've succeeded in learning some Russian.

But, I digress . . . Madame von Meck was a great admirer of Tchaikovsky and for many years she generously subsidized his work and even, his private life. The only condition that Madame had placed before Tchaikovsky was that he would *never try to meet her*. Tchaikovsky had dedicated much of his work to her, but he had never met his benefactor face to face and had never set foot in her golden Salon! Why? It is a mystery, which I hope someday would be solved.

Because of that strange edict I had never met Tchaikovsky, either. I always regretted that I was not the one to introduce his remarkable *Concerto #1 in B-flat* to the public. I've heard that the director of Moscow Conservatory, Nicholas Rubinstein, to whom the concerto was dedicated, declared the concerto *'unplayable and worthless.'* Rubinstein refused to play it. I learned many years later, that Rubinstein changed his mind after the concerto had tremendous success at its premiere not in Russia, but of all places, *in Boston*, in America! Rubinstein had second thoughts about it and performed the concerto at the Paris Exhibition in 1878 to great acclaim. Good for him, I thought.

Even though I had never met the great composer I new his music very well. It was constantly played or sung in the von Meck mansion. My Claude too, had contributed to the Tchaikovsky cult by transcribing for the piano several of his orchestral compositions. Madame especially admired Debussy's piano arrangement of the selections from Tchaikovsky's ballet *The Swan Lake*. She wrote to the composer for his permission to have the arrangement published. Claude was delirious with happiness. He became a *published* composer.

I could see that Debussy was well liked by the members of the family. The children tried to teach him Russian and I began to learn it also, since the improvised lessons were taught between piano sessions. The children enjoyed the hilarious mistakes that Claude made trying to learn their difficult language. Their laughter would often bring Madame into the room. Soon she began to call Claude "my little Frenchman", or *"Petroushka"* and finally, *"Bussyk"*, which was an endearing nickname made out of his last name-*Debussy*.

Encouraged by this atmosphere of friendliness, gaiety and riches, I noticed that Claude began to change. He put on the airs of a sophisticated man of the world, not realizing that his charm was in his youth and innocence. He began to smoke and I often thought that I would suffocate in the thick clouds of tobacco fumes as he sat composing, a cigarette in the corner of his mouth, the ashes falling on my keyboard.

"How old are you Bussyk?" Madame asked him one day.

"Twenty," Claude said without batting an eye.

"Twenty?" Madame repeated, her face expressing disbelief. Later, I heard her laugh as she told her guests that her *Bussyk* could not have been more than sixteen.

"So, what did he accomplish with this stupid lie? Why did he add two years to his real age of eighteen?" I thought never being able to comprehend human logic.

I caught him lying again when he pretended that he was a graduate of Paris Conservatory and the winner of a piano competition. Why did he lie? Why did he want to impress his employer with the accomplishments not yet achieved? Why do humans lie? We, the musical instruments, we never lie. A false note is a false note.

After a few weeks in Moscow, Debussy once again became obsessed with composing. Madame came upon him unexpectedly as he was scribbling in his music notebook with one hand, while striking my keyboard with another. "What are you doing, *mon petit?*" she asked bending over his shoulder.

"Oh, Madame, I did not hear you enter . . ." Claude jumped to his feet. "I am writing a trio . . . I beg your forgiveness for using the Salon," he muttered, looking at his feet, his face crimson. "And there is more . . .

"What is it?" she put her hand under his chin, forcing him to look at her.

"You're so kind Madame . . . I've abused your kindness . . . I lied to you," he finally blurted out. "I still have three more years to study at the Conservatory. And I did not receive the first prize at graduation—since I have not yet graduated. And I . . ."

"And you are *not twenty years old*," she finished with a chuckle. "How old are you?"

"Eighteen," Claude said, looking miserable.

"Eighteen . . ." she repeated pensively. "Just because you are *eighteen* and because you had courage to admit your lies, I forgive you." She stretched her bejeweled hand to him and Claude kissed it fervently.

"Oh, Madame, how can I ever thank you!"

"You can dedicate your new composition *to me*," she said as she regally sailed out of the room, her silk skirts rustling.

Encouraged by the kind words of his patroness, Claude plunged into his work. I too, did my best reproducing the melodies that were still only in Claude's mind. In a few days we completed the trio and Claude presented it to Madame Von Meck.

The *Trio in G major* was performed at one of her soirées by her household musicians violinist Pachulsky, cellist Danielenko and my Claude. I must confess, it bore little resemblance to the future compositions of my master that had made him immortal.

Autumn was approaching and it was time for Claude to leave Madame von Meck's household. I presumed that I would be placed on the train also for a return trip to Paris, but to my grief, Claude decided to leave me behind. Madame offered to buy me, to relieve him of the responsibility, and Claude sold me, without a second thought. I was deeply hurt. I *loved* the boy!

"How could he?" I thought bitterly. But Debussy left and I became one of several household instruments. Madame would show me to her friends, saying, "This is my *French* piano," stressing my nationality, just as she did with her *German* piano and her *American* one.

I thought that I would never see Claude Debussy again, but the following summer he reappeared among us once more.

SIX

"Bussyk has arrived!" the children shouted as they ran down the marble staircase to greet Debussy. I heard the noise at the entrance, shrieks of laughter and then the voice that I knew so well proclaiming that it was good to be back. My strings vibrated imperceptibly; I had not forgiven his disloyalty, but I waited anxiously for our first encounter. Did he miss me? Was he able to compose just as well with some other piano or did his work suffer because I was not there to support him? I saw his reflection in the mirror as he ascended the stairs. He had not changed much. The same sturdy frame, the same shoulder-length hair, forming a leonine mane around his young face, the usual touch of green in his clothing, He burst into the salon and flung a portfolio of his new works on a chair next to me.

"How is my good old friend?" he exclaimed caressing me. "I missed you, old boy! My new piano is *nothing* compared to you." His praise completely wiped out my bitterness over the past few months. I responded to his fingers with my usual eagerness, foreseeing hours of harmonious work together.

The children laughed. "You talk to the piano as if it were a person!"

"To me it is even better than a person. To me it is the soul of my soul . . ." Claude said seriously.

"To me, also," Sonya agreed quietly. She came into the room unnoticed by anyone and now stood on the other side of my keyboard. Debussy stared at her as if he were stunned. Sonya has changed. Her gangling arms were gone, along with the reddish hands of adolescence. Her face was clear of pimples and shone with good health. At sixteen, Sonya had become a real beauty. She was my only solace during the long, dark months of the Moscow winter when she would come to the salon for her singing lessons. She did learn *Violetta's* arias and I gloried in her light and easy coloratura soprano. I wondered, would she be allowed by her mother to become an opera singer? I knew that Russian aristocracy did not tolerate *professional performers* among their ranks, but Madame von Meck wasn't an aristocrat. She was a widow of a merchant. Would she encourage her daughter's talent? I worried about Sonya. Her talent should be developed for the pleasure of many and not be limited by singing at her mother's soirées. Ah, what an old fool I am! I had the same feelings for Sonya that once I had for Solange and then for Jacqueline. Am I destined to fall in love with every pretty girl that crosses my path?

I spent many happy hours with Claude and Sonya. I watched how their friendship grew into love and I witnessed their first kiss. And it was I, who had heard their plans about marriage. Just like so many years ago, with Jacqueline and Bernard!

"You must ask Maman for my hand," I heard Sonya whisper to Claude. "But wait until she's in a good mood. You know how difficult she can be." Claude knew very well the capriciousness of his patroness. She suffered from insomnia and often stayed awake deep into the night. She demanded that Claude entertain her by playing compositions of her beloved Tchaikovsky. I knew that Claude would have loved to introduce some of his own work, but Madame seemed to be enchanted by Tchaikovsky.

Debussy began to detest Tchaikovsky. I remember how once he expressed his annoyance with Tchaikovsky's habit of using peasant songs in his compositions. "To me, as a *cosmopolitan,* these primitive melodies sound monotonous," he declared with youthful arrogance.

"How dare you! How dare you to criticize the *divinity!*" Madame left the salon in a fury. She stopped talking to Claude for a week after that episode. Debussy knew very well how dangerous it could be to catch her in a bad mood.

He and Sonya waited for an opportune moment to declare their intensions. Then, one evening, in my Green Salon where Madame liked to sit when there were no guests, Claude and I played for her a new *Barcarolle,* by Tchaikovsky, of course.

Madame was enchanted by the new composition. She kissed Claude on his forehead, declaring, "You are such a talented pianist, my Bussyk!" The kiss was probably meant for Tchaikovsky, but Debussy felt emboldened. He thought that it was an opportune moment to ask for Sonya's hand.

Blushing to the roots of his wild hair, he burst forth in a resolute voice, "Madame, Sonya and I love one another . . . We would like to get married. Please, give us your blessings."

Madame von Meck slowly rose from her chair. Her face became blotchy with anger but she remained composed. "You must be joking Monsieur," she said icily. She did not call him "Bussyk" anymore. "What *right* have you to think that I may allow such *misalliance!*"

"What right?" Debussy objected, deeply wounded by her arrogance. "There is no better right than the right of our love for one another. Ask Sonya. She will tell you that she loves me and wants to marry me. Ask Sonya."

"I will do no such thing. Sonya is only sixteen and she will marry someone whom *I* will choose for her."

"But she loves *me*!" Claude cried in anguish.

"Rubbish!" Madame snorted. "Sonya will forget you in a week. As for you, Monsieur Debussy, your employment with me is terminated as of this moment. You'll be paid fully for the whole summer, but you'll leave for the railroad station *at once*. Your luggage will be sent to the train. Goodbye, Monsieur". She rang the bell and her secretary appeared at the door.

"Escort Monsieur Debussy to the railroad station immediately," she ordered coldly. "If there is no train for Paris today, put him on any train leaving for any place in Europe. Stay with him until he leaves. He is not permitted to see anyone of my family or to leave a message to anyone." The secretary bowed and with a gesture invited Claude to follow him.

With his head hung low, his face red with humiliation and anger, Claude followed him.

"I will not permit a penniless musician to worm his way into the heart of an heiress!" Madame screeched, finally loosing self-control.

Debussy left. I never saw him again.

Sonya soon forgot him. Within a year she was married to a wealthy man, many years her senior, and I had become a part of her dowry. I was moved into Sonya's mansion and the years of dull, sleepy life followed. Sonya hardly ever sang or played piano anymore and when she did—she used another instrument, as if she deliberately avoided me. I stood neglected, alone in the big, cold, seldom used salon. I was out of tune but no tuner was sent to keep me in shape.

Ten, maybe even more years had passed . . . No one cared for me. Only the chiming of clocks in the big, joyless house enlivened the monotony of my life. The clocks would strike one by one, room by room, as if by some special plan they were spaced minutes apart. They created a strange symphony of sound as some of them boomed, the others chimed, still others tinkled every quarter of an hour, starting at one end of the house and ending somewhere in the service quarters. This seemed to be the only melodic sound in the gloomy mansion.

Sonya grew thin and irritable. I wondered if she ever thought of Debussy. As his fame grew and his name became synonymous with the music of France, did Sonya ever regret that she did not follow her heart and marry her first love? I never knew.

Then I heard from the chambermaids that Sonya had sold her house along with the fine furniture to a man who had a yacht that he sailed in the Black Sea. The man was an eccentric. Although he owned several houses in Russia and in Europe, he lived on his yacht.

Soon our house was full of packing cases. Chairs and tables were crated, Persian rugs rolled, paintings and mirrors packed in padded boxes. Finally, I, too, was crated for shipment to Odessa on the Black Sea.

"That yacht must be enormous to be able to accommodate a concert piano," I thought as once again I found myself riding in the baggage car of a train. I have seen engravings of sailboats in the Debussy household in Paris but none of them looked large enough for a grand piano. I was facing this new phase of my life with trepidation; to be aboard a sea-going vessel, to live on *water*? I shuddered at the thought of damage the salt air would do to my strings and my elegant wooden case. But, alas, as usual, I had no power over my own destiny.

We arrived in Odessa in the early morning. As I rode on the platform of a flat cart pulled by two draft horses, I caught a glimpse of this southern city, slumbering lazily in the rising sun. Some buildings and monuments reminded me of Moscow and even Paris, but my main impression of Odessa was that of a provincial city, charming, but probably, dull. We rode along a wide boulevard under the leafy chestnut trees, the horses' hooves making precise sounds like a percussion instrument, echoing in the deserted streets. Once in a while we would encounter quaint two-wheeled carts, filled to capacity with watermelons or cabbages. The carts were dragged by small fuzzy donkeys, which strained in their harnesses pulling the heavy loads. Quaint flat-faced and slit-eyed men dressed in loose multi-colored garments reaching to their ankles, drove the carts. With their heads clean-shaven but covered with embroidered skullcaps, they had scraggly drooping moustaches and thin, goat-like beards. They were the Tatars. As I was to learn later, the Tatars once were the powerful nomadic tribes, which for two and a half centuries terrorized Russia. They even made inroads into Central Europe and threatened Vienna. What could have been the fate of Europe if Tsar Ivan IV, the Terrible, the same one who had built the Cathedral that so fascinated me, had not defeated the Tatars? It was hard to imagine that these peaceful men, dozing on the tops of their carts were the descendents of the fierce warriors of Genghis Khan.

As we approached the harbor, a light breeze moved the corners of the tarpaulin that sheltered me from the sun. A magnificent panorama of the harbor and the shimmering sea studded with white sails of pleasure boats spread before me. In the distance I could see the dark-gray silhouettes of naval ships at anchor in Odessa. Somewhere among those many vessels in the harbor, was the yacht *Renaissance* that was soon to become my new home.

I was lifted from my cart by a crane. It lowered its huge arm and picked me off the cart as if I were a child's toy. Effortlessly, the crane swung over and deposited me aboard a flat barge. A sooty tugboat, which was attached by ropes to the barge, gave three deep-throated hoots and we were off. Through the cracks in my packing case I could see that the deck of the barge was crowded with familiar pieces of furniture from Sonya's house. It made me feel a little better; I was not going to be the only stranger aboard.

The tug pulled the barge into the open sea. The air felt fresh and salty. I could hear harsh cries of the seagulls as they followed in our wake. The water was a brilliant sapphire-blue color and I wondered why was it called the *Black Sea?* It took me some time, before I realized that the name was appropriate: the sea *was* black during storms, so *black* that it made me think of ink.

The *Renaissance* was a huge, gleaming motor yacht, anchored far off shore. I have heard that it was second in size only to the *Standart,* the Russian Tsar's own great motor yacht.

The *Renaissance* had a crew of sixty who began to unload us from the barge to the decks. They chanted some barbaric-sounding rhythmical shanties as they worked, which I thought would have amused Claude Debussy.

The master of the *Renaissance,* Count Sergei Roumiantzev, stood on the captain's bridge observing the unloading of his treasures. I noticed that he was in his middle years, corpulent and very tall. His hair was steel-grey and cut very short so it bristled like a brush. He had an enormous grey moustache that sprouted under his fleshy nose like an ornamental bush. He was dressed in immaculate white trousers and a dark-blue tunic with gold buttons and fringed epaulettes. He looked like an admiral and perhaps, he was an admiral. He exuded strength and good health and his voice was a deep booming basso, so typical of Russian men. I liked him.

I was uncrated and moved into the grand salon, a large room on the main deck. At once the count placed himself in front of me and began to play a lively polka. He was a bad pianist. He banged my keys loudly, carelessly striking wrong notes, but he played with such obvious pleasure that I forgave him the rough treatment and the absence of talent.

Loud music brought into the salon a handsome old lady dressed in a rustling black silk. "Enough of this wild noise!" she cried in French, pretending to be horrified.

"I am sorry, Maman. You obviously don't appreciate my virtuosity!" the count retorted. "But it did bring you out of your cabin!"

The old countess made a wry face as she fitted herself into an elaborately gilded chair from Sonya's house. She squirmed and fussed in it, like a hen, making a lot of unnecessary movements before settling down and folding her hands on her lap. "I still don't like it," she said stubbornly, apparently resuming the previous argument. 'I think that it was foolish to throw away perfectly functional furniture and substitute this . . . this . . . *"confection"*! It just doesn't belong on the boat. Besides, it is not very comfortable."

The count smiled a patient smile and stood up. "You are right, Maman, but my fiancée *insisted* that I refurbish the yacht. You know that I would have preferred to keep the old furnishings, but she proclaimed them atrocious."

The old countess pursed her lips. I could see that she must have disapproved not only of the furniture but of the forthcoming marriage as well. "I still insist that wicker furniture, such as our Emperor has on his *Standart*, is appropriate to a sea-going vessel, while these *confections* are good only for a lady's boudoir," she insisted, still calling the furniture "*confections*". I wondered whether she would call *me* some derogatory name as well.

A few days later I made my acquaintance with my future mistress. She was brought to the *Renaissance* by a small navy cutter. She stepped aboard looking annoyed, surrounded by three or four young chambermaids and ignoring the young officer who helped her along the gangway. She looked Italian to me. She had velvety-dark eyes and gleaming black hair. Her beautiful features were cold and arrogant, her manner haughty. She examined the *Renaissance* closely and proclaimed that it was much more to her taste now, without "that ugly wicker furniture." The old countess barely spoke to her. I could predict that there would be many clashes between the two of them.

The young woman ran her fingers over my keys and said that I would do, that I was good enough. *Good enough*! I was burning with indignation. If I only could, I would have shouted that the great Liszt, the incomparable Saint-Saëns and the fabulous Debussy caressed my keys and praised me, while she . . . who was *she*, anyway? I was suffocating with anger!

Count Roumiantzev ordered the *Renaissance* out to sea for a short sail. I heard the sound of running feet as the crew darted in all directions to fulfill his orders. The white sails were unfurled. Even in the salon I could hear the canvas snap as the wind filled the sails. The boat slowly turned and moved with the wind. The count and his fiancée and even the old countess went on deck and I was left alone to experience my first sea voyage.

The boat moved smoothly over the waves and at times I had the impression that we stood still. "It's much more enjoyable than a train journey," I thought. Of course, on the train I was always locked in a baggage compartment, encased in a packing crate, resting for hours on my side. Here, on the boat, I was in the familiar surroundings of a salon, standing on a lush Persian carpet. "Quite a difference," I thought.

When the *Renaissance* returned to her moorings the count's fiancée was pouting. She did not enjoy the outing. She complained that she felt seasick. "I want to go back to Moscow," she announced.

"If you wish" the count quickly agreed. I could see that my master had acquired a master of his own.

"I'll stay aboard while you're in Moscow. I love sailing," the old countess said. "My doctor advised me to rest in the sea air, and I would rather stay on the boat than in my hotel in Odessa."

"Of course, Maman. Capitan Polzunov will be at your disposal. He'll take you for a sail whenever you like."

"Wonderful! I enjoy sailing! I might go to Yalta for a few days and visit Her Majesty at Livadia Palace." The countess kissed her son good-bye but nodded to her future daughter-in-law. I heard the crew lower a lifeboat and the count and his fiancée with her maids were on their way to shore.

Again I was neglected like a piece of unnecessary adornment. How I missed Paris and the humble flat of Debussy! How I missed Claude, who grew before my eyes from a child prodigy into a world-renowned composer! I even missed Madame von Meck's family with her children, all learning how to play piano, or harp or violin! How unfair it was to waste me on a boat where no one appreciated me, while there were hundreds of young people who needed me desperately! What an unforgivable waste!

SEVEN

I stood forlornly in the salon. I was bored, thinking unkind thoughts about the rich, who seemed to saturate their surroundings with possessions for which they had neither love nor need. My only diversions were the daily visits of the cleaning crew who dusted the furniture and swept the floors chatting and gossiping about the events on shore, keeping me aware of the life outside my floating prison.

It was 1905, the year of Russia's defeat in war with Japan. Russians apparently were badly beaten by the Japanese and the country suffered national humiliation. I, who had witnessed the popular uprising in Paris following the defeat in the Franco-Prussian war, was not surprised when I heard about the possibility of a revolutionary uprising in Russia. And, it happened. The peaceful Odessa and its picturesque harbor were suddenly shaken by a fantastic event. One of the naval vessels of the Black Sea Fleet, the battleship *Potemkin* mutinied!

From our anchorage we could hear gunshots. My strings vibrated at the familiar sound and I even felt pain from the wound that I carried for over thirty years.

Listening to the heated discussions among the crew, I learned that the storm on the *Potemkin* had been brewing for a long time; it took an egregious incident to blow it into a full-fledged mutiny.

It all had started when the sailors of the *Potemkin* were served beet and cabbage soup made with rotted meat. The sailors refused to eat the *borscht* even though the ship's doctor supposedly checked the meat and approved it. The captain ordered the crew for a roll call on quarterdeck. He demanded that the instigators of the revolt step forward. No one did. Outraged by such obvious disobedience, the captain ordered the crew to return to the mess hall and eat their *borscht*. The sailors stood their ground and refused.

Captain Evgeny Golikov must have lost his head. He had ordered the Marines on deck to face the sailors. A company of armed Marines appeared on the deck. The captain again demanded that the instigators step forward. Once again, no one obeyed.

"Aim!" Golikov ordered. The Marines aimed their riffles at the sailors. Some sailors began to waiver, many breaking away from the group and returning to the mess hall. About thirty sailors remained, not believing that the captain would give an order to shoot.

"Fire!" the captain shouted.

"Brothers, no! Don't shoot! We're your brothers! Don't shoot!" the sailors yelled. The Marines hesitated. One of them lowered his riffle. Then another, and another. They refused to carry out the monstrous order.

Realizing the seriousness of the situation Captain Golikov grabbed his own revolver, but it was too late. The sailors, joined by the armed Marines, turned on their officers.

I do not know how many people were killed or thrown overboard. I heard that the hated captain Evgeny Golikov was killed and so was the ship's doctor, who had approved the rotten meat as fit for consumption. The ship fell into the hands of the mutineers. They raised the red flag of the revolution on the topmast, inviting the rest of the Fleet to follow their example.

The public imagination was fired by the incident. Immediately the students of the Odessa University organized a delivery of fresh produce to the sailors of the *Potemkin*. Boats of every description, from sail yachts to rowboats and one-oar kayaks, were loaded with watermelons and vegetables, fresh meats and eggs and began their race to the *Potemkin*. I could see this instantaneous armada from the large windows of the salon. It seemed to make the calm sea boil from the wakes behind dozens of boats.

The old countess Roumiantzev also watched the drama from the salon sitting at the window not far from me. I heard her sigh and whisper, "Dear Lord, what's going on?" She pulled a bell cord to summon our captain.

Presently, captain Polzunov appeared before her, immaculate in his summer whites, respectful, yet, full of his authority.

"You wished to see me Your Highness?"

"Yes, Captain. Please sit down." She indicated a chair next to her. The captain obeyed, squeezing himself into an uncomfortable little chair from Sonya's collection. "Do we have enough food on board?" the countess asked.

"Oh, yes, plenty. Enough to feed an army!" The captain smiled.

"In that case, I would like to send some of it to the *Potemkin*."

The captain was startled. "You must be joking Your Highness," he said, standing up. "The crew of the *Potemkin* is a mutinous, rebellious band, killers of their officers!"

"They are still Russians, like you and me. Mind you, I don't condone the murder of their officers, if it is true. But I am sure, the sailors acted in self-defense. After all, they were not armed, isn't it so?"

"Yes." The captain had to agree.

"So, you see, they had to defend themselves against those who had fired at them. Some men were killed, isn't it true?"

"I suppose."

"Well, those who survived will need food. I want you to send our extra food to the *Potemkin*. Poor souls will have a very short time left to enjoy life. The Tsar will punish them for their revolt. They will be arrested. I want to make their last few days a little easier for them."

"Yes, Your Highness." The captain bowed.

"Also, I would like to send a message to the sailors," the countess continued pensively. "Something reassuring . . . Something like—*'don't despair, God is merciful. The prayers of the Russian people are with you!'* Can you do that for me?"

"Certainly, Your Highness!" He clicked his heels, bowed to the countess and left. At once a series of bright little flags began to climb up our tallest mast, spelling the message of the old lady to the sailors of the *Potemkin*. The countess, with a satisfied expression on her wrinkled face, rang for tea.

I heard a faint sound from the bowels of the boat as our auxiliary engines began to throb. Soon the anchors were lifted and the *Renaissance*, with its sails folded, began to move, its engines working at a low speed. We inched our way ahead but were unable to get close to the battleship; the sea around it was virtually cluttered with small boats. I could hear our captain ordering to lower two lifeboats. Our men loaded crates of food and barrels of water into the boats and rowed away toward the *Potemkin*.

As the boats returned to the yacht, the *Renaissance* began to maneuver for the return to her anchorage. This time I could clearly see the city from the starboard window of the salon. It was an unforgettable sight. It looked as if the whole populace of Odessa was crowded on the embankment. The famous Odessa steps, a long stretch of broad stairs that led from a high street above, to the sea below, were teaming with people who came to cheer the *Potemkin*. Here and there I could see bright splashes of red flags as people poured down the steps. Suddenly, there were new faint sounds, which were almost obliterated by the clamor of our engines. Again I recognized the sounds. I heard them before in the days of the French Commune. They were the sounds of gunfire.

The people on the steps panicked. I could see how they ran, trying to escape the advancing soldiers who had appeared on the top of the stairs. The soldiers presented a solid wall, moving slowly down the steps, sweeping the crowds before them, their fixed bayonets glistening in the sun.

"My God, what are they doing?" the countess, who had watched the scene from the same window, cried in anguish. We saw several people fall, remaining motionless on the steps. The advancing soldiers moved forward relentlessly, stepping over the fallen bodies. Soon it was all over. The steps were cleared of the crowds and only a few dead bodies marred the sweep of the majestic staircase. A few more shots were heard from the harbor, the dead bodies were removed and then, it was quiet again.

I learned later that the *Potemkin* was blockaded by the ships of the Black Sea Fleet and ordered to surrender. The crew refused and sent an invitation to the Fleet to join in the rebellion. One small *Torpedo Boat # 267* accepted the invitation and raised the red flag.

The Commander of the Fleet ordered the guns of the ships to be turned toward the rebels and be ready to fire. The crews of the Fleet refused to obey.

To prevent even more trouble, the Fleet Commander wisely decided to lift the blockade and let the *Potemkin* and the torpedo boat escape to near-by Rumania, where the Rumanian authorities immediately interned both vessels. The Rumanian government repatriated the mutinous sailors back to Russia, where they were promptly jailed and then exiled to Siberia. Thus, the old countess was right: the sailors did not have much time to enjoy their freedom.

The count was furious when he returned to Odessa and learned about his mother's action. "You have compromised me, Mother!" he stormed. "What explanation can I give to the Tsar when he hears about your escapade?"

The old lady shrugged her shoulders. "No harm was done," she said. "All I have done was to send the poor lads some food and water . . ." But the count was implacable. He suggested that his mother should return to her hotel in the city, and the old proud lady left without another word. I never saw her again. I didn't see much of the count either. He and his bride came aboard the *Renaissance* only two or three times between the *Potemkin* incident in 1905 and the Bolshevik revolution of 1917. When they finally came to Odessa again, it was to escape from Red Russia forever.

EIGHT

O dessa and the rest of the Crimean Peninsula were the last bastions of the White Russian contingents that fought the Red conquerors. As the Red forces gained strength, the Crimean ports became the final points of escape for thousands of defeated Whites. From our anchorage in Odessa I observed hundreds of people swarming down the steps, along the promenade, spilling down to the beaches in hope of being taken to a place of safety, away from the advancing Red armies. Some were able to buy a passage on the ships bearing foreign flags that sailed away overloaded with panicked Russian refugees.

By contrast, our yacht was an example of order and discipline. Although we lost most of the lower ranks of our crew to the revolutionaries, Captain Polzunov still had enough men to sail the *Renaissance* across the Black Sea, into Turkish waters.

Among the escaping passengers were count Roumiantzev, his wife and their four young children. Captain Polzunov's family of eight and the wives and children of the remaining crew, still loyal to the count. The latter group was kept below decks so I had never met them. It seemed that even in adversity, Russian aristocracy insisted on segregating themselves from common people.

The *Renaissance* weighed anchor at night, hoping to slip through the Red blockade that was tightening its grip around the Black Sea ports still in the hands of the Whites.

We glided out of our mooring without lights, with only one of our engines providing minimum power. As soon as we cleared the harbor and nosed into the open sea, the captain ordered full speed ahead. Sails were unfurled and the engines began to throb to maximum capacity. The *Renaissance* took to the wind like a magnificent huge seagull, skimming the waves in quest of Turkish shores.

Count Roumiantzev worked as a stocker alongside the few remaining loyal sailors. He looked tired and old, his clothes soiled with grease and coal dust. Had I not known who he was, I could have taken him for one of the enginemen.

A heavy shroud of tension hung over the yacht. I could feel it in the very air and it suffocated me with fear. What would become of us?

Over the hum of our engines I heard several booming explosions. The Red fleet began its bombardment of Odessa. It was the third time that I heard this ugly, terrifying sound of exploding artillery shells. The first was during the French Commune in the 1870. Then came the rebellion on the *Potemkin* in 1905, and now, the Russian Civil War. I knew very little of what was happening in Russia. From the conversations between the count and the captain, I had learned that Russia was engaged in the World War. I did not know that there was such a war. Sometime later, I learned, that in 1917 the Tsar had been overthrown, put under arrest and the proletarian republic was proclaimed. My master, count Roumiantzev immediately joined the White Guards, the armed opposition to the Red republic. The Reds murdered the Tsar and his entire family, thus removing the rallying cause for the Whites who were fighting for the restoration of the monarchy. Many bloody battles of the Civil War were fought between the Reds and the Whites, until the Reds were finally in command of the country. The defeated Whites and their families were forced to flee for their lives.

My master had no alternative. Were he to remain in Russia, he would have been shot by a firing squad like tens of thousands of other aristocrats and even common people who opposed the new regime.

The count was fortunate: he had his own means of transportation to take him into exile, while most of the hapless multitudes that I observed on the beaches had no means of escape. The sad, disorganized people were left to face the grim reality of the defeated—imprisonment and death.

I was fascinated by the heated political discussions in the *Renaissance* salon. I adopted the attitude of total neutrality toward the Red revolution. I considered myself *French* even though I had lived in Russia for many years and became fluent in their language. But I was *French*, and proud of it. I felt that it was none of my business to get emotionally involved in Russian internal struggles. Yet—I could not help but be excited to bear witness to historical events of such magnitude.

I suppose, were my relations with the count and his arrogant wife any warmer, I would have taken their predicament more personally. As it was, I hardly knew them. They expressed no affection for me and though I felt sorry that they had to flee their own country, I was already looking forward to my new masters; I had heard that the count was going to sell his yacht when we had reached a foreign port.

The telephone rang. I was intrigued with this invention that permitted people to converse with one another over great distances, even from one city to another. I watched my master as he listened to the captain's report from the bridge.

The news was bad. The Reds were in pursuit. "Two torpedo boats are after us," the count said. "I must go to the bridge, but you, women and children, lie down on the floor and stay there. Turn the lights off . . . We'll try to outrun them . . ."

The women and children threw themselves on the floor, crawling between the chairs and the tables, some of them crowding under me in their effort to hide. We heard the rapid staccato of machine gun fire as the bullets ripped into our hull. Powerful beam of light suddenly illuminated our fleeing vessel, making every object stand out sharply outlined in its cruel brightness, emphasizing the look of terror on the blanched faces of women and children cowering on the floor. It reflected in the mirrors, creating an unbearable brilliance. Several more bursts of machine-gun fire hit the boat, but the *Renaissance* continued her flight skimming the water like a mythical sea bird.

Gradually, we began to gain on the pursuers. When they realized that they could not intercept and capture the yacht, the Reds tried to sink it. They fired a torpedo, but it missed us. The *Renaissance* continued her flight, vibrating from her agonizing exertion. A second torpedo missed us as well.

The pursuers fell back. The harsh lights were extinguished. We became invisible.

I heard the footsteps and the count entered the salon groping his way in the black vacuum. "They are gone," he said in a low voice as if the Reds could hear him. "We should be out of danger soon, unless they send faster boats and better gunners to sink us!"

I shuddered and my strings gave forth a pitiful little 'ting'. "What a tragic ending for an innocent by-stander!" I thought in selfish despair.

The night passed. There were no more enemy boats in our wake.

The sun rose slowly over the horizon coloring the clouds and the sea in hues of crimson and orange. The wind was brisk and the surface of the water was alive with sea caps, pink from the rays of the rising sun.

The captain and the count examined the damage to the ship. They found scores of small holes in the outer hull and one large gaping cavity on the portside. The crewmen climbed up the rigging and although the canvas was partially torn by the machine-gun bullets, the sails were still serviceable. The vital sections of the vessel remained undamaged. We stayed on our course for another twenty-four hours without interference from passing ships of foreign nations, who recognized our flag and wished us good luck, but offered no assistance in our flight.

My spirits rose. We were probably out of danger. In another day, we sighted Constantinople, later known as Istanbul, the magnificent jewel of a city on the Bosporus, where Europe meets Asia across a narrow strait. The skyline of Constantinople was one of the most fantastic sights to behold. Through the large windows of the salon I watched as the panorama of the fabled city with its tall minaret towers and graceful cupolas of stately mosques spread before me. In the crisp air of early morning I could see the brilliant colors of the tiles and the intricate designs of the lacy stone carvings of the slender minarets. The battered *Renaissance* sailed into the harbor at the Golden Horn and dropped her anchor.

Over the din of the harbor I could hear some wailing sounds as muezzins called the faithful to their morning prayers. How I wished that I could explore this exotic city of a Thousand And One Nights! As it was, I had to be satisfied with my restricted view of Constantinople through the window.

At high noon a small boat bearing red and white flag with the Turkish emblem of a crescent and star, secured itself at our portside. Several uniformed officials wearing red fezzes with black tassels climbed aboard. They spoke good French as they presented the count with the internment papers for his boat and the passengers.

Count Roumiantzev and his family, together with captain Polzunov and his wife and children sat down for a minute to say a silent prayer as was the Russian custom before undertaking any prolonged journey. Then, making the sign of the cross, they followed the Turkish officials to the small boat.

It was the last time that I saw my Russian owners. The count sold the *Renaissance*, complete with its furnishings, to an American millionaire, Carter Rowlings III. As I learned later, the passengers and the crew of the *Renaissance* were eventually granted asylum in Turkey, but count Roumiantzev and his family preferred to make their way to France, where they settled in Paris, my native city.

My new owner, Mr. Rowlings closely examined the yacht. At once he ordered to start the necessary repairs. I was moved to some dingy storage along with the rest of Sonya's furniture, which was sold to a hashish-smelling dealer. Surprisingly, I was not sold. Did it mean that Mr. Rowlings wanted to keep me? I did not know. I felt sad parting company with my old friends, all those delicate French chairs and tables whom I first met in Madame von Meck's house when I was still young, but I was relieved not to become the property of that hashish-smelling dealer.

The *Renaissance* spent six months in dry-dock where she was repaired, repainted and renamed. The new owner changed her noble name into the

Swanee Queen. He refurbished the salon in the modern style, with tables and leather chairs riveted to the floor. I was the only one left from the items belonging to the *Renaissance.* The new furnishings looked impersonal and I doubted whether I would be able to establish friendly relations with that group of factory-made items.

My sorrow at parting from my French friends was somehow minimized by the anticipation of a new adventure and a long voyage to the United States, for it was our destination.

From the beginning I disliked Mr. Rowlings. He smoked big black cigars and dropped ashes all over the place. I dreaded the time when he would drop ashes on me! He talked in a very loud voice, which I found annoying. Perhaps I was unjust to Mr. Rowlings because I did not understand his language. It was easy before. The upper class Russians spoke faultless French. Being of an inquisitive mind, I learned Russian as well and became quite fluent in that difficult language, but now I faced a huge gap in communication. My master and the *Swanee Queen* crew spoke only their own language, which was English.

We sailed from Turkey through the Bosporus into the sea of Marmora and passing through the Dardanelles entered the Aegean Sea. We circled slowly among the Greek Islands stopping often at different islands for a few days. Mr. Rawlings was a collector of antiquities. In every port or even at some modest moorings, our *Swanee Queen* was always surrounded by dozens of small boats bringing fragments of marble statuary and pottery, or chunks of masonry decorated with mosaics. My new master bought everything. Soon the yacht's storage groaned from the weight of broken columns, noseless marble gods and armless goddesses. Even in the grand salon every available inch of space was soon filled with his crated treasures.

Needless to say, no one touched my keyboard. I suspected that no one would. Mr. Rawlings did not impress me as a music lover.

We spent several months cruising the Greek Islands. Despite my loneliness, I enjoyed it. The weather was glorious most of the time and the views from the salon windows were breathtaking. On the island of Rhodes we picked up two passengers who were to accompany us as far as Lisbon. To my great joy, they were *French*! Once again I was able to understand what was happening around me. The new passengers were Charles Dupont, a professor of Archeology from the Sorbonne University and his protégé Pierre de Mourville. The young Pierre served as an interpreter between the professor and Mr. Rawlings. I was delighted. My dull existence among the crates was over. Professor Dupont spent his entire days in my company, in the salon, cataloguing Mr. Rowlings' purchases. He immediately rejected most of the acquisitions as worthless, while he praised the others and handled them with reverence.

Pierre made himself indispensable. He talked to Mr. Rawlings in rapid English, translating back and forth Professor Dupont's remarks and Mr. Rowlings questions. He reminded me of Bernard, my young composer from the French Commune days. He had the same wiry build; the same curly dark hair and sparkling dark eyes that made him look like a Sicilian boy from a popular postcard. But while Bernard was sickly and listless, Pierre burst with robust health and good humor.

Little by little the crates in the salon were thinned out. Professor Dupont was ruthless in sorting Mr. Rawlings acquisitions. With no thought of the money spent on worthless objects, Mr. Rowlings had them dumped into the sea. Pierre jumped with joy like a boy as the fakes were thrown overboard raising geysers of water.

"Someday archeologists will find these fakes and believe that they have discovered a lost civilization!" Pierre laughed.

"By that time, the junk will become the *real* antiques and they won't be too far off," replied the professor. With the salon cleared of cargo, life became quite pleasant for me. Every night Mr. Rowlings and his two guests gathered in my company to drink cognac and talk about archeology, antiquity and mythology. Professor Dupont was well versed in these subjects. He willingly shared his knowledge with Mr. Rowlings (and me), with the help of Pierre's translations.

The old professor captivated me. He was an ugly-looking man, short and stout, with a hump on his back and a huge pendulous nose. He was almost bald and his protruding ears stood out like the wings of a butterfly, pink and translucent. But ugly as he was, he was kind and his mind was brilliant. There was a touching father-son relationship between him and Pierre. The handsome young man obviously admired and revered his old mentor, working diligently with him on the catalogue of the antiquities, and doing many menial chores for the old man, such as shining his boots or sewing a button on his coat. But for me, professor Dupont had another priceless asset. He was a *musician!*

As soon as the salon was cleared of Mr. Rawlings' superfluous purchases, professor Dupont made his way to my keyboard. I was ashamed of myself for I was out of tune, but the old man caressed me with his gnarled fingers and declared me a treasure. Despite my shyness I sang with joy. Every evening from then on, after the work was done, the professor, who knew by heart a lot of classical piano repertoire, entertained Mr. Rawlings and Pierre. Feeling ecstatic, I gave forth the music of Chopin and Liszt, of Tchaikovsky and Schubert.

One night, professor Dupont announced that he would like to play something written by his friend, a famous French composer, Claude Debussy. The composition was called *Clair de Lune*. When I heard Claude's name I almost jumped with joy on my three fat legs. Claude Debussy! My little genius, whom I helped to achieve international fame! And to think that professor Dupont knew him! Oh, to be able to tell the old man that I, too, was Claude's friend, one of his *first* friends, one of his most devoted ones. Alas! I could express my feelings toward my erstwhile friend only through the music that he wrote and I was to sing.

Clair de Lune was exquisite. My Claude captured in music the elusive sorcery of the moonlight, the melancholy of solitude and the beauty of the shimmering night. If one could be in love with a piece of music, *Clair de Lune* would be the object of one's infatuation. Even the rowdy Mr. Rawlings was impressed with Debussy's composition. "I bet, he wrote it for some dame!" he said puffing on his stinking cigar. Pierre translated his remark to the professor and the old man smiled.

"Yes," he said. "Debussy was madly in love with a certain Madame Vasnier. He was a very young man then . . . A boy, really . . . Madame Vasnier was the wife of a distinguished architect, years older than her admirer, so I think there was not a chance for Debussy's passion. Nevertheless, I think he wrote *Clair de Lune* for her. It was long time ago . . ."

"He must've written it after he left me in Russia and returned to Paris," I thought. I recalled how Debussy was dismissed by his Russian patroness, Madame von Meck. His unfortunate interlude with her daughter Sonya, obviously did not keep him from falling in love with someone else shortly after. His young heart was full of unrequited love, which allowed him to create this tender composition. Good for him, I thought. Pity that I wasn't *the piano* on which he created that exquisite piece. It probably was my imagination, but I thought that I heard some familiar cords in it, something that Claude had been experimenting with ever since his youth.

Several evenings later professor Dupont entertained us with the tales about mythological gods and goddesses, whose marble heads and torsos he catalogued during the day. As we approached the straits of Gibraltar, which separated Europe from Africa, he pointed to the steep rock and said, "Here stand forever the pillars of Heracles."

Mr. Rowlings immediately wanted to know what the old man meant by his remark. "*Alors*, the ancient Greeks believed that Heracles passed this way in his quest for the oxen of Geryon . . . It was Heracles tenth labor. The myth tells us about the hero's combat with the three-bodied winged giant Geryon, with his shepherd Eurytion, and their two-headed dog. Needless to say, Heracles slew them all. But apparently, our hero had trouble in finding the place where those giants lived. Remember, they had no maps in those days."

"Where *did* they live, those horrible giants?" Mr. Rowlings inquired with a chuckle.

"They lived on the tiny isle of Erythea. You can find it on some old maps. Anyhow, when Heracles reached the straits, where we are now, the heat annoyed him. Without thinking, he shot an arrow at the sun, which of course was one of the Olympian gods and thus—sacred. But Phoebus Apollo, the god of light, was an admirer of our hero, so instead of punishing him for his impudence, he gave him his own boat that steered Heracles across the water, right to the isle of Erythea."

"So, what happened then?" Mr. Rowlings was obviously interested in the professor's story.

"To commemorate his crossing from Europe to Africa, Heracles erected two tall pillars—the Pillars of Heracles, which became known in modern times as the Rocks of Gibraltar. As for our hero, he loaded his stolen oxen in the magic boat and escaped."

"It must have been quite a boat—to have all those cows aboard!" Mr. Rowlings laughed.

"Yes, that's the beauty of mythology. Nothing was *impossible* for those heroes. Nothing!"

"So, our hero Heracles was a criminal? He stole the cattle from the giants and expropriated Apollo's boat. Some hero!' said Mr. Rowlings. "He was a hood!"

"Oh, but he returned the boat. He knew better than to steal from the Olympian god. However, you're right. If you look at mythology from our point of view that is, from the twentieth century point of view you'll find that the heroes were all cheats and thieves and liars, especially, the greatest hero of all, Heracles. He was brave and strong but very cunning. In many ways, he was stupid, too . . . Read about him when you have time. You'll enjoy the tales. By the way, in Roman mythology, he was known as Hercules."

"This guy fascinates me. I surely will read about him when we get back to the States!" Mr. Rowlings exclaimed.

I could've listened to Professor Dupont's tales forever, but as usual our voyage came to an end. We arrived in Portugal.

Our yacht was to be unloaded and all its precious cargo reloaded on an ocean-going freighter. The *Swanee Queen* was to be dry-docked for necessary repairs before undertaking the long voyage across the Atlantic. I wished that professor Dupont would play *Clair de Lune* before leaving the boat, but the old man was busy supervising the transport of antiquities from one vessel to another. Music was the last thing on his mind. Reluctantly, I turned my attention to the gleaming city beyond the harbor.

Lisbon, observed from the water, was truly, beautiful. Right in from of the harbor I could see a large square surrounded by stately colonnaded buildings that I thought might have been palaces. In the center of the square rose a bronze monument to some king or famous explorer astride a rearing horse. I wished I knew something about Portuguese history, but as you know, I have never attended school.

Beyond the monument I saw an archway through which a stream of carriages and motorcars poured into the square. It was high noon and the citizens enjoyed perfect weather and the fresh breeze from the sea. As the streets of the city climbed up and away from the harbor I could see an old craggy castle on the top of the hill. Oh, to see a real medieval castle at close range! To explore it, to walk on its ramparts! Alas, it was not ever be for me.

The cargo was unloaded and professor Dupont and Pierre bid goodbye to Mr. Rowlings. I watched as they crossed the gangplank leading to shore and almost immediately disappeared in the milling crowds. Once more I reflected on the fragility of the chance encounters: one met people only to never see them again . . . how sad!

The repairs on the *Swanee Queen* were minor and within a month she was ready to sail, like Columbus, for the New World. Mr. Rowlings and his crew of twelve navigated the huge yacht with no seeming effort. And to think that Count Roumiantzev barely managed with the crew of sixty! But Russians were known for their waste of manpower: in the galley alone, the count employed ten cooks.

We sailed from Lisbon and set course for the Canary Islands. I liked that name. I wondered whether the islands were named after the little yellow birds whose intricate coloratura singing I admired so much. I remember how many, many years ago, in Paris, when I was still young and a member of the Matignon household, I heard a canary sing whenever Solange practiced her scales. The little bird, whose cage was hanging in the window near-by, always joined Solange in a duet. Sometimes the bird's singing would become too persistent and I wished that he would stop, but the little creature loved singing and continued his trilling just for the joy of it. Being an artist myself, I understood his need to perform. I learned to tolerate his trilling.

Reminiscing about my past I almost missed the first sight of the Canary Islands as they rose suddenly out of the morning mist. There were seven of them, rocky and volcanic, presenting to us their picturesque harbors and tiny villages. A fleet of fishing boats crowded their harbors and one could see several foreign ships refueling in the hospitable waters. The *Swanee Queen* lowered her sails and we slowly made our way into the harbor using auxiliary power.

Almost at once our yards were commandeered by hundreds of chirping birds, incessantly arguing for their places on the rigging. Through the windows of the salon I observed these nervous, pretty creatures, which seemed to be incapable of remaining still or keeping quiet. Were they the relatives of the little canary I once have known?

We remained in the Canary Islands only long enough to replenish our supply of fresh water before undertaking the long voyage across the Atlantic Ocean, the voyage I would rather forget about for we were plagued by violent storms.

On the very first night after we left the Canary Islands, we were caught by a sudden squall. Wind seemed to surround us from every direction. Mr. Rowlings ordered the crew to shorten sail, batten down the hatches and secure the objects throughout the ship. Fortunately, all the furniture in the salon was permanently bolted to the floor, that is, except me. At first, my sheer weight kept me from sliding, however, as the wind increased and the yacht listed sharply, I felt my small wheels move under me. I rolled across the floor and crashed into the wall. Before I was able to gather my senses and right myself, the ship listed in the opposite direction and I rolled again, crashing into the opposite wall. I rolled back and forth, smashing myself against everything in front of me, breaking the stationary furniture and mirrors in my clumsy helplessness, like some hippopotamus gone mad. The wind whistled about me, sometimes sounding like a pitiful infant, sometimes howling like a lost dog or thundering like an artillery explosion. Through the plate glass windows I could see the angry waves beating at the ship with demonic fury. Chandeliers broke away from their chains and tumbled to the floor, their prisms splintering into thousands of sharp fragments.

When after three days the storm had finally subsided, the salon was a shambles. Mr. Rowlings spat at his feet, but said nothing as he took an inventory of the devastation. I felt embarrassed for causing so much damage, but what could have I done in time of such great calamity? It was lucky that the yacht had a steel hull, or I would have crashed through its walls and ended my days on the bottom of the ocean, with fish swimming among my strings and the mermaids running their green fingers over my keys.

The deckhands tied me down with stout ropes to the three huge bolts hastily driven into the floor. And none too soon, for another storm hit the wretched vessel. Torrential rains washed over us, flooding every open space.

We were pursued by hurricane-force storms for several more days. I was sure that Mr. Rawlings was sorry now that he chose to sail the yacht with such small crew.

When at last the sun peeked from behind the clouds pregnant with rain and the winds had died down, the men fell on the deck, exhausted by their ordeal. Mr. Rawlings remained at his post on the bridge. I had to admit that he was an excellent skipper. He saved us from almost certain death by his expert handling of the vessel. I had to admire a man of such heroic qualities.

We by-passed the Virgin Islands and the Dominican Republic and entered American waters. Our sails were badly torn but they were still serviceable. Mr. Rowlings was probably in a great hurry to reach the port of New Orleans in the Gulf of Mexico for he stopped neither in Cuba nor in Miami, which both lay on our way. He kept his course toward New Orleans.

I did not care anymore. I was too exhausted by my bouts with *mal-de-mere.* I would not be surprised if my fruitwood body had turned green from seasickness. I wanted to be in port, especially, in the French-speaking port of New Orleans.

NINE

About a couple of weeks after we docked at New Orleans, Mr. Rowlings ordered his crew to remove me from the yacht, which was to be repaired and furnished with new crisp sails. He wished to install a more suitable instrument in my stead. I took too much space in the salon, Mr. Rowlings said. This so-called *'more suitable instrument'*, proved to be *a player piano.* I have never been so insulted! To be considered "*unsuitable*"? The greatest composers and pianists *praised me!* To replace *me* by a mechanical toy? Really! To add more insult to my injured pride, Mr. Rowlings did not even bother to sell me. He simply declared that I was beyond repair, being too badly scratched and battered. He ordered to remove me from the yacht and let anyone cart me away.

I was pushed down the gangplank, dragged across a lading platform and left standing in the middle of a long stretch of sandy beach. A crowd of curious black children surrounded me. One or two of them timidly pocked at my keys, while the others jumped on my top and sat there, all in a row, like a flock of little cheery birds. They dangled their dusty bare feet and traced the carved trim of my case with their dirty fingers, sticky from licorice candy. Toward the evening the lading platform and the beach became deserted. Even the children left, their interest in me gone as suddenly as it was aroused.

I looked with longing at the yacht that for so many years was my home. She was so near! I could clearly hear my successor, the upright player piano grinding some simple melodies, as if laughing at me. "This time it is the end of me," I thought grimly. "Who is going to find me here, on the deserted beach of a private harbor? I will stand here until I disintegrate and become a nesting place for seabirds."

The night fell, a humid, warm night, full of smells of the sea and sultry scents of sub-tropical vegetation. But I barely noticed the velvety warmth of the night in the stupor of my desperation. "This time there will be no miracle. No one is going to save me," I thought forlornly.

The ravished *Swanee Queen* stood close to me, her torn sails drooping. She reminded me of a picture of *The Flying Dutchman.* Madame Von Meck had a piano score of Richard Wagner's opera, with the picture of the ghostly ship on its cover. She often played the brooding melodies from the opera or sang the part of Senta with Claude's accompaniment.

The memories of my former patroness, whom I disliked, were sweet to me now. "How well she took care of me!" I thought. "How she cherished me . . . How she loved music!"

My bittersweet reveries were interrupted by a strange creaking sound. I saw an old wagon pulled by a mule, moving slowly over the beach. Three black men and a boy sat in the wagon and it looked as if they were coming straight toward me.

"Here it is Gramps," I heard the boy say in a high voice. "What did I tell ya?" By now I knew enough English to understand simple conversation. A happy premonition seized my heart. *I would be rescued,* I just knew it! The old man stopped the mule a few feet away from me and climbed down from the tall seat of the wagon.

"Are you sure, sonny, that the captain said he did not care who gets this *pee-ano*" he asked the boy.

"I swear it, Gramps! That's what he said 'I don't care who gits it. Just git it off my boat,'" the boy cried eagerly. If I could talk, I would have corroborated the boy's story, for it was exactly what Mr. Rowlings had said, only he had added a few swear words to his command.

"Well in such case, let's git this *pee-ano* on the wagon and git going." Two other men joined him on the sand and after a few minutes of puffing and sweating and straining every muscle of their powerful bodies, they loaded me on the wagon. The old man climbed back on the driver seat, while the younger men walked behind the wagon, holding me, helping the mule drag me off the beach and away from the yacht. The boy scurried behind the party, sweeping the tracks with an old broom in case Mr. Rowlings had a change of mind and decided on a different and more profitable way of disposing of me.

Soon the yacht, the beach and decades of my life were behind me. I was entering a new phase.

My new master, *"Fancy Fingers"* Jake Jenkins was an unusual man. He was old, thin and wiry like a circus performer. He was black but the palms of his hands were pink. His head looked almost round with its tightly curled short hair touched with grey. He and his friends cleaned me and patched me up, and Jake himself tuned me. He could not read music but he played piano with the virtuosity of a concert performer. His nickname, *"Fancy Fingers,"* suited him well, I thought. When he played, he bent his head close to the keyboard, as if trying to touch it with his face, while his nibble fingers flew in fancy combinations of intricate harmonies and rhythms. My keys would steam up from his hot breath. I could not help but admire his genius.

Jake Jenkins was a *jazz* pianist. Never before had I participated in creating such interesting syncopations and wild harmonies. Jake had three more musicians performing with him: a trumpeter, a saxophonist, who also played a clarinet, and a contrabassist, who played an old scratched bass fiddle by plucking it. They played by ear, improvising as they went, creating some new combinations as they changed from one key to another. It was pure joy for me to be part of this unusual group. What perfect command of their instruments they had! What perfect sense of music!

Jake installed me on the tiny stage of a smoky cellar. Every night the room filled with jazz lovers, who came to the nightclub to listen to Jake and his group, to drink forbidden whiskey and to dance. The women wore short dresses, well above their knees, a far cry from the gowns worn by the ladies at Madame von Meck's soirées with their bustles and corsets and tons of diamonds and pearls. Most of the women were black and young and pretty and they sparkled with cheap necklaces that looked like Christmas glass beads. As I discovered later it was New Orleans tradition to throw glass beads from the balconies down to the milling crowds. A charming tradition, I must say! Especially, during Mardi Gras celebrations.

Every night I vibrated with untamed, improvisational, never-the-same music that was *jazz*. I *loved* it!

During the several years that I worked with "*Fancy Fingers*" Jake, I made my acquaintance with many great jazz musicians, who often came to New Orleans from Chicago or New York or St. Louis to listen to Jake. They inevitably got up on the stage and played for hours with Jake's group. Thus I met Louis Armstrong, and Fats Waller, Bix Beiderbecke and Duke Ellington, whose composition *Sophisticated Lady* was one of my favorites. I heard Duke himself play, his handsome face with its puffy eyes, looking dreamy. "You've got a great piano, old buddy," he told my master. "It's a real treasure." I could have wept with joy if I were a human. I was appreciated again!

Those years of making jazz music in the cellar of New Orleans were among the most exciting years of my life. But as usual, a new disaster sprung upon me, like a thief crouching in the darkness waiting for an opportune moment. Old Jake died.

The nightclub was closed as the musicians prepared for Jake's funeral. I detest funerals, remembering vividly the death of Bernard so many years ago in Paris. But again, as in Paris I was to participate in the funeral of my master: this time I was to be a member of the solemn procession as well.

It was a bright spring day, the first one I had seen in several years, for I lost all sense of changing seasons, or even of the time of day. It was always dark in the nightclub.

I was moved out of the cellar and pushed over a ramp onto a platform of a truck festooned with black crepe and American flags. In front of the truck stood a long black limousine inside of which I could see a coffin containing poor Jake's remains under a pile of flowers.

The members of Jake's band climbed on the truck platform and a young man who sometimes substituted for Jake at the piano began to bang on my keys *When the Saints Come Marching In.* The musicians picked up the melody. As they played, more musicians joined the procession. Some of them jumped on the platform, the others fell in step with the marchers. Soon this improvised orchestra swelled to several dozen players as the limousine began to move, our truck behind it. The musicians played, swaying and dancing as they followed us. The dense crowds watching the procession from the sidewalks clapped their hands, sang and danced, even when the musicians switched to solemn spirituals, such as "*Swing Low, Sweet Chariot.*"

There were hundreds of black men, women and children who followed our slow moving cortège, singing with joyous verve, as if they wished to speed good ol' Jake to the next world. The *celebrated* Jake, instead of mourn him. I liked that.

From the top of the truck I could see people on the sidewalks, black and white, taking their hats off and making the sign of the cross. Jake was well known and respected in New Orleans.

We continued to play. The crowd shouted *Hallelujah* and swayed until we reached the gates of the cemetery. The limousine and several dilapidated cars with Jake's family and close friends entered the gates and the musicians carried the casket with Jake's body to the gravesite. The crowd followed, still singing and dancing.

I knew that there would be a change in my life, now that Jake was gone. Sure enough, Jake's widow had to sell me to cover the expenses incurred by his illness and funeral.

My new master was a *Syndicate*. At first, when I heard the word "*syndicate*", I imagined a portly, well-groomed gentleman, by the name of Mr. Syndicate. To my surprise, Mr. Syndicate proved to be not a man but a group of men involved in a business enterprise, known collectively as the *Syndicate*. This enterprising group was the owner of an old steamboat, a side-wheeler, which used to ply the muddy Mississippi River during the last century. The Syndicate renovated the old vessel, the *Daisy-Lou,* furnishing her lavishly in the style of *La Belle Époque.*

I was restrung, tuned and moved to the grand salon, which was decorated in red velvet with gold tassels and fringes. I presumed that I would be happy in my new habitat floating up and down the river, were it not for one serious complication: the *Syndicate* decided to paint me *red,* to match the décor. My exquisite fruitwood case and lids were sandpapered, which was quite painful, and then, I was covered with several coats of shiny red enamel paint. I glistened like a Chinese lacquered box.

On the opening night the salon on the *Daisy-Lou* was full of people in evening clothes. The women wore tiny dresses, well above their knees, their hair cut short, like little boys, their lips painted red and their eyes outrageously outlined with black paint. But they were pretty as ever, all these American girls, who came to dance to my music aboard the *Daisy-Lou.*

As I switched my attention to the men, I had to admit that they did not change as drastically as the ladies. Although their bushy beards and exuberant moustaches were gone, the men looked much the same as they looked some fifty or sixty years ago. In their evening clothes they still reminded me of penguins.

It took me a few days to realize that *dancing* was the least important activity aboard the *Daisy-Lou.* The main activity was gambling and drinking, which was against the law. Unbeknownst to me, I found myself in the midst of a group of criminals breaking the law every minute of the day or night. *The Syndicate* that I respected as a conglomeration of businessmen was nothing but a bunch of crooks! I would have blushed in shame at finding myself in such despicable company, but of course, I was already permanently *red.*

For several months the *Daisy-Lou* steamed up and down the Mississippi, its tall chimney spewing dense clouds of black smoke, its side wheels splashing the brownish water of the wide river. Every night the air around the *Daisy-Lou* was full of music and laughter as people carelessly parted with their money.

Then, one night the Federal agents raided the boat. Her days as a glamorous lawbreaker were over. No one realized that among the crowd that boarded our gambling ship at Natchez were dozens of special agents, whose sole purpose was to catch the *Syndicate* in action. The agents were dressed in evening clothes like any other wealthy patrons who nightly crowded the gaming tables below decks.

On the upper deck in my salon, the younger crowd danced the *Charleston,* as usual. Suddenly we heard a loud noise coming from the gaming rooms below.

A few shots were fired. I heard hysterical screams of women and the sounds of running feet as some patrons tried to escape. But where could they escape? The *Daisy-Lou* continued indifferently on her course along the river. I saw several members of the *Syndicate* dive into the dark waters of the river and I hoped for their sake that they were strong swimmers, for the Mississippi was a wide river.

By early morning all the gamblers were rounded up in the upper salon, their wrists handcuffed behind their backs. The agents looked very different now: with their jackets removed, they exposed their shoulder harnesses with guns resting in holsters. They quickly separated the lawbreaking gamblers from the innocent dancers who had become trapped in the raid. The captain was ordered to head back to Natchez. As we approached the landing, I saw a row of police vans waiting for the arrested passengers. One after another they entered the vehicles, the members of the *Syndicate* among them.

The *Daisy-Lou* was finished. The Federal government closed the illegal operation and confiscated the ship. We were towed to a small bay in the delta, where we were locked and sealed by special seals. We remained under lock for several months while the authorities decided what to do with us. Finally, the furnishings and equipment were sold at public auction and the *Daisy-Lou* was dismantled for scrap.

A traveling dance band pooled its resources to buy me. With my garish red paint peeling off, my strings slack and some even broken, I was squeezed into a dilapidated yellow school bus with all its seats removed to accommodate me. This school bus and its seven musicians became my home and family for the next several years.

The leader of the band was Pete Walker, a huge black man who played drums. He had enormous hands, which seemed to fly in the air with incredible speed as he manipulated the drumsticks, striking various cymbals, bells, drums and turtle shells. In spite of his threatening countenance, Pete was a gentle soul. I had never seen him being angry or mean, even during the most trying days of our gypsy lives. Pete's younger brother, Larry, was a pianist, and he became my new boss. Like *"Fancy Fingers"*, Larry played entirely by ear, and his style reminded me of Jake's. And no wonder: I recalled seeing young Larry in the dim nightclub, rapturously following Jake's syncopated improvisations. Now he was all grown-up, developing his own style. There were five other black musicians. They all lived in the bus, sleeping on the floor among the assorted musical instruments. They took turns driving, just as they shared their earnings, which I presumed to be very meager, for my masters were always half-starved.

But what great music they produced on their beat-up instruments, these seven men who could not read music!

My memory of those lean years is one long chain of small towns, where we played one-night stands in school gymnasiums or Elk Lodges. Summer or winter, our yellow bus rolled along, its sides emblazoned with crimson lettering *Pete's Dixie-Land Jazz Band*, through which one could still see the black letters spelling *School Bus.*

Pete and his men built for me a sturdy triangular frame with wheels at each of its corners. They nailed me to it so that it would be easier for them to move me and set me anywhere, be it a rough cement of a parking lot or a small stage of a high school.

The monotony of our wandering lives was regularly interrupted by the bus' breakdowns, when the vehicle had to be unloaded on the side of the road and the musicians would become mechanics, trying to fix their conveyance with bits of wire and duct tape or spare parts picked-up or snatched somewhere along the way. Our dream destination was Hollywood, California, where the musicians hoped to become famous and rich working in the movies.

But it was only I, who had finally made it to Hollywood. However, it was still way out in the future.

Town after town passed through my memory, month after month, year after year. I remember the endless, dusty roads of the Midwest, the poor dilapidated farms, and the boarded-up stores . . . America was in the midst of the Great Depression. My seven masters felt the hard times even more acutely than the rest of the citizens. There were weeks when we had no engagements to play, no one-night stands, no weddings. The men tried to find some other jobs to tide them over the bad times, but it was hopeless. The whole country was suffering and the roads were full of wanderers, all in search of work.

We lost two men who decided to return to New Orleans. They hoped to wait out the cruel times working on small farms, living with their families. They hoped that at least there would be enough to eat. They jumped aboard a freight car, waving to us as the train pulled away.

The remaining five took to stealing. Whenever we passed a farm, Larry would somehow manage to bring in a chicken or a few eggs. In the summer the men raided orchards or dug up a few potatoes from some field on the outskirts of a farm.

They played impromptu concerts on the squares of some dusty prairie towns, dragging me down to the hot asphalt. Pete would put his battered old hat on the ground hoping to collect a few bucks from the listening crowd.

Very seldom our take was more than a dollar in small coins. Obviously the band could not survive much longer in that way.

Then—a new craze seized America and revived the optimism of my five remaining masters. This new obsession was called *Marathon Dancing*. Even the little towns were staging these affairs, where couples were competing with one another for prize money. The competition was based on the length of interrupted dancing and the endurance of the participating couples. The promoters collected admission fees from the spectators who would watch and bet on their favorites.

Pete's Dixie Land Jazz Band was engaged by a Kansas City promoter to play for a marathon dance contest in some small town, the name of which escapes me, for all towns looked the same after so many months of wandering. It was the test of endurance for the musicians as well, for we were to play for as long as there were contestants to dance.

Pete parked our bus on the dirt-covered back lot of a local school and I was pushed onto a specially built little platform in the school gym. I was intrigued by this new twist in my long career. From the top of my platform I could see about a hundred couples, with large cardboard numbers pinned on their backs, ready to begin the competition.

The sleazy promoter ascended the platform and through a megaphone announced the rules of the contest. "Ladies and gentlemen," he yelled. "There will be three prizes for the three couples who remain on the floor the longest. The first prize is one hundred dollars; the second prize, seventy-five dollars, and the last one, fifty dollars. Every two hours there will be a ten-minute break. So, good luck, and God bless you!"

Pete rolled the drums and the marathon began. From my spot on the platform I could observe a sea of human flesh, moving shoulder to shoulder in a vigorous foxtrot. The bleachers were full of spectators who paid a dollar each to watch the dancers.

The first two hours seemed to be easy, although several middle-aged couples gave up and retreated to the bleachers. The majority of the contestants were back on the floor at the sound of the bell announcing the end of a rest period. Pete's men, too, returned to the stand hastily gobbling stale sandwiches and gulping cups of hot coffee.

The second two hours began to show on the contestants in several dramatic ways. Some women fainted and had to be carried off the floor. The others just quit, realizing that their stamina was gone. Pete's men too, felt the enormous tension of continuous effort. They began to play slower, taking less time on their solo *"rips,"* not caring anymore for the applause of appreciation.

The people on the bleachers must have been having a good time. They came to the marathon contest with their whole families, like to a picnic, bringing with them baskets of food and bottles of beer, cheering their favorites and booing the quitters.

The third two-hour period had only about a dozen couples, still able to dance. I watched their drawn, grey faces. They were exhausted. They moved their legs heavily, stubbornly enduring pain in their quest for prize money. My five masters did not fare any better. Pete's shiny black face looked ashen and Larry's nimble fingers barely moved on my keyboard. Soon Larry's head began to nod as he fought with fatigue, trying to stay awake. Mercifully, the bell rang, announcing another ten-minute respite. The musicians shuffled backstage where they collapsed on the floor, instantly falling asleep. The dancers, too, staggered to the sides of the floor, collapsing like wooden puppets when their strings had been suddenly let loose.

Too soon the bell rang again. One couple limped to the floor. The others were still sprawled on the benches, unable to move. The musicians barely stirred.

"Get up, you black dogs!" the promoter swore, kicking savagely with his two-tone shoe at Pete's sleeping form. "'I ain't paying you for sleeping!'"

The musicians stumbled back to the platform. The fourth period had begun.

"Now, the real fun begins!" the promoter yelled. "Ladies and gentlemen, place your bets on your favorites! Which couple is going to go home with a hundred bucks? Here's your chance to make some dough for yourselves! Place your bets! There are only ten couples left! Choose your winners!" Over the sound of our dissonant music I could hear the noise of the crowd making bets.

Meanwhile the foot-weary robots continued their mechanical movements. The partners clutched at one another for support lest they become disqualified if one or the other lets go. Somehow, another two hours went by. The musicians stupefied by exhaustion, did not even leave their seats; they fell asleep instantly. Larry's head fell heavily on my keys, making me utter a loud discord under its weight.

For the fifth period there were only ten dancers left. "Okay, ladies and gentlemen, here is your last chance to make some dough!" the promoter shouted again. "Only five couples left! Place your bets, ladies and gents, think of this like a horse race! Make your bets, to win, to show or to place! Yawsuh!" he yelled as the bell rang again.

The remaining five couples shuffled to the dance floor. I could not tell anymore whether they were young or middle-aged. They looked ancient, their faces gaunt, and their eyes glassy in their deep, dark sockets. Their legs refused to hold them up, buckling under them as if they were the legs of folding chairs. But tenaciously, they hung to one another and to the bright promise of prize money.

The crowd was growing wild. People jumped to their feet, yelling, whistling, and egging their favorites to go on. In the last few minutes of the fifth period, one couple collapsed, a woman crying in pain, her ankle badly sprained. The couple was hastily removed from the dance floor, while the remaining four couples continued their mechanical movements, without the slightest reaction to the accident. I thought that probably their minds were fogged by physical exhaustion to the point of stupor. The bell rang, proclaiming the beginning of the respite. The couples seemed not to hear it. They continued to move, even though the music stopped.

"How do you like them zombies?" the promoter yelled, laughing. "They just *love* to dance! They ain't gonna stop for nothin'!" Someone tapped the dancers on their shoulders and pointed to the benches where they could rest. They collapsed on the benches like heaps of wet rags.

Another bell announced the last period. The three couples dragged themselves back on the floor.

Pete and his boys began a cacophony of sounds, which had no recognizable melody or tempo. The dancers moved doggedly, shuffling in one place, barely moving their feet. I think, they did not realize that they were already the winners of at least fifty dollars. But they kept going, hoping for more. The time crawled with maddening slowness.

"Give up," I wanted to shout. The promoter yelled in Pete's ear to liven up the tempo, but the drumsticks kept falling out of Pete's tired hands and his foot, beating time on a large drum, kept skipping the beats, soon to stop altogether. At last, one more couple collapsed. A shout rose to the rafters of the gym as the crowd went wild with excitement. It would take only minutes now and the winner would be declared. The two couples moved round and round in clumsy imitation of dancing. Finally, a man stumbled over the feet of his partner and the couple fell to the floor. The promoter declared the remaining couple the winners.

"*The winners!*" he shouted, raising their arms high as if they were prizefighters.

The monstrous marathon was over. The crowd began to disperse amidst the curses of those who had lost their bets, happy shouts of those who had won, no one paying attention to the emaciated dancers on the benches or musicians who remained motionless as if they were in a coma. The fun was over.

Pete's band received fifty dollars for its super-human endeavor of twelve hours of continued playing. I heard the promoter brag to some local politician that he had cleared for himself more than four thousand bucks!

We played several more similar marathons in different towns, but I was never able to get used to the barbarity of the spectacle. The inhumanity of the competition was as cruel as the sports of the ancient Romans about which I have learned from professor Dupont during my stay aboard the *Swanee Queen*. What terrible anguish and emotional damage these couples must have suffered in their quest for a few dollars!

Somehow, my five masters managed to scratch enough money for another year, going up and down the country roads never getting closer to Hollywood and the big money. Finally, even the optimistic Pete, our drummer, had to admit that the band had no future. There were too many unemployed musicians traveling about the country, competing with one another for a few dollars, besides, with the popularity of radio, the best jazz music became available free of charge. The traveling bands were finished.

To make matters worse, our bus had finally broken down. It fell apart so completely that the boys had to abandon it, without even trying to repair it. I watched sadly as the musicians unloaded the bus until only the bulky drum set and I remained inside.

Pete decided to dissolve his group. "What shall we do with the *Eighty-eight*?" Larry asked using the nickname he gave me because of my eighty-eight keys.

"We'll sell it," Pete said. "And we sell the drums. We sell it and get back home. We should've gone back long ago, to our *Big Easy* . . ." he added bitterly. I felt deep sympathy for this giant of a man and his big dream of reaching California and becoming famous. He was a good musician. They all were good musicians, and yet, here they were with their spirits broken, their hopes shattered, their pockets empty, sitting on the side of the road, next to a broken bus.

"Who's going to buy our stuff in this God-forsaken place?" Larry said with a sneer.

"The High School, that's who. They can always use a piano and a good set of drums," retorted Pete.

"Yeah, for how much?" challenged Larry. I could see that he did not want to part with me.

"Fifty bucks."

"Fifty bucks! You must be kidding. We bought the piano for *sixty!*" Larry yelled. "And your drums! You paid more than twenty-five for them in New Orleans!"

"Beggars can't be choosers," said Pete. "We have no choice, boys, we can't drag these heavy instruments around without a bus. We must take what we can get. Fifty bucks is better than nothing." Larry continued to protest the cheap sale, but even he had finally to submit to the brutal reality.

A flattop truck arrived. Two husky high school boys helped the musicians to load me and the drum set on the truck. Larry turned away his handsome black face as the truck pulled away. I thought that I saw tears in his eyes. He truly loved me, this poor, uneducated young man, who had a God-given talent.

TEN

Several uneventful years passed. I stood in the corner of the stage of a high school assembly hall, wheeled in the center of the stage on my dilapidated triangular platform for occasional Glee Club presentations. They were the same presentations, one year after another, only with different singers. It was a comfortable life, but oh, so dull! I wished that there were *someone*, who could make me sing again, or explode in fortissimo, displaying all my abilities, which so many famous artists had appreciated! Alas, in the small mid-western farming community the best musicians were the self-taught banjo players.

I knew very little about what was happening in the world. I was astonished one day to learn that the world was engaged in a global war. A loud speaker was installed in the assembly hall and every morning the students and the teachers would gather there for a radio broadcast of the latest news. Thus I learned about the fall of my native country, France, and about the invasion of Russia by Germany. Finally, early in December 1941, I heard the chilling news that America was attacked by Japan in the Pacific.

Immediately scores of young men enlisted in the armed forces. I could barely recognize the former students, now trim soldiers, who came to bid good-bye to their Alma Mater.

The tempo of life in town had changed over night. The school assembly hall became the hub of activity. Regular patriotic meetings were held in my presence, each starting and ending with the crowds singing patriotic songs with my accompaniment. I did my best to sound vigorous and optimistic. I too, was patriotic, feeling very *American!*

When after four years the Second World War ended with our victory, the assembly hall was used for a joyous celebration. One after another our soldiers returned home. Not all of our soldiers. Many were claimed in battle on foreign soil. The returnees looked grown-up and serious, many of them maimed, many still suffering from wounds, but all intoxicated with victory. Among them was Robert Wright, the town's favorite, whom I remembered as one of the soloists of our Glee Club. Bob, as I remembered him, had always been a good-looking boy. Now, after four years, he had become a magnificent young man. He was tall and broad-shouldered, wearing proudly his sergeant's uniform decorated with several colorful ribbons. He looked like a movie star, which was exactly what he wanted to become.

The town greeted Robert as a hero. A special *Robert Wright Day* was proclaimed and a dance was held in his honor. Bob arrived to the assembly hall with the prettiest girl in town, obviously enjoying the adulation of his fellow-citizens. He sat on the stage dais under the American flag, led the crowd in the Pledge of Allegiance and sprinkled his conversation with French words. He was among the Americans who liberated Paris and he wanted everyone to be aware of it.

Our Glee Club presented a program of familiar songs and Robert was coxed to sing solo. After the thunderous ovation for their favorite soldier, Robert modestly returned to his place on the dais. "I see you still have this ridiculous red piano!" he exclaimed turning to the school principal. "You should get an electric organ!"

"Yes, we should, but we don't have any funds for such an expenditure," the principal said.

"I'll get you one," Robert said with aplomb.

"This piano is not bad. It just needs to be refinished and properly tuned. It comes from a very famous French piano factory," the choir director came to my defense.

"*French*, you say?" Robert suddenly became interested. He stood up and walked around me, scratching the horrid red paint with his fingernail here and there, to see what was beneath the cracked surface. He struck a few chords and peered closely inside my case.

"I'll tell what," he said to the principal. "Let's swap. I'll get you a brand-new electric organ if you give me this old piano. I did not realize that it was French. It will remind me of Paris."

The principal eagerly agreed. "Sure, take it, Bobby! It's been too cumbersome for us anyway, and we would rather have a new electric organ!"

The next day Robert made arrangements to have me moved into the parlor of his parent's small house. Immediately he began to remove the ugly red paint from my body. He worked on me for weeks, using his entire furlough until I stood stripped of all color, totally *naked*. However, Robert reached an *impasse* in the next step of his attempt to restore me: who was going to change my strings, refinish me and tune me in this small backwater town? I already thought of it, but I did not reckon with his plans for the future. Robert Wright was going to become a movie star. It was his ambition ever since he was a boy and took part in school theatricals. Were it not for the war, Robert might have been unable to fulfill his ambition, forever staying in a small town, dreaming of glory and stardom and big money. But now he was a war hero, his pockets were stuffed with saved money, his good looks fully matured, his speech sprinkled with French words. Robert had a very good chance of succeeding.

He left me, still unfinished, in the care of his parents as he took off for Hollywood. Within a year he sent for me, for Robert Wright became a huge success with his very first film.

I was taken to a piano repair shop straight from the railroad station and I did not see Bob for another half a year. It took a long time to get me into shape. I was badly hurt through the years of neglect and adversity. When I was finally rehabilitated, restrung and tuned, I looked even better than ever. My carved fruitwood case was shiny again and my cracked ivories replaced. My three legs acquired new small wheels and the ugly triangular platform to which Pete's jazz musicians nailed me was discarded. My new strings were ordered from the *Salon Pleyel* in Paris and I felt *French* again!

A special piano-moving padded truck drove me to Bob Wright's palatial residence. As I rode along Hollywood Boulevard toward Bel-Air I could not help but reminisce about my life and its many vicissitudes. So much had happened during my lifetime! I lived through two world wars and three revolutions . . . I met the richest of the land and I lived with the poorest . . . I met the famous and the infamous . . . I saw radio, automobile and motion pictures became indispensable parts of people's lives. And what about the aviation! The world went from Gambetta's clumsy balloons to slick jet planes that screeched overhead! I had seen it all. The thought occurred to me that I ought to make my experiences available to everyone. I wished that I could write my memoirs.

Bob Wright's new residence was in the hills of Bel-Air, the most fashionable section of Los Angeles. I could not imagine how anyone would become so rich in such a short time, but there he was, standing in front of an imposing French-styled chateau, waiting for me. He was dressed in an expensive cowboy outfit made of the softest suede. His boots were intricately tooled and traced with silver. On his hip was a low-slung belt, encrusted with silver and two guns with ivory handles. "Are they the *real* guns?" I wondered. A tall ten-gallon white cowboy hat was tilted just off his face as he stood, squinting in the sunlight, watching the movers unload me. He was smiling, but his eyes looked steely-blue and cold on his sun-tanned face. He has changed, I thought. I knew in an instant that his phenomenal success was not accidental, but rather the result of a precisely calculated campaign. I knew that Bob would not let anything or anyone interfere with his goals. My intuition about him proved to be correct.

I was installed at the focal point of a large, handsome room completely devoid of furniture. Bob walked around me, his footsteps sounding loud on uncarpeted floor. He ran his hand along my glossy case, a smile of satisfaction on his face. Then he put on his sunglasses, lowered the shades on the tall windows and left the room. It was weeks before I saw him again.

I stood in the darkness of the empty room, but there was no bitterness in my heart. Through the years I grew wise and stopped worrying about situations over which I had no control.

When I saw Bob again, he appeared in the company of a short man who was dressed in a loud Hawaiian shirt and Bermuda shorts, his protruding abdomen threatening to pop the buttons of his shirt. Next to Bob he looked ridiculous, but I noticed that my master listened to him with respect.

"I'm telling you, boy, you've got to live up to your *image*!" the man was saying poking at Bob's muscular chest with a pudgy forefinger. "You're an *American Cowboy* and not some sissy foreigner! You know what that means? You must live on a ranch; you must have horses, you must ride broncos and rope cows! Instead, what do you do? You go to Berlitz School to study *French*!" he lisped with derision. "*Parlez-Vous Français?*" he mocked. "You sunk all your dough into a mansion for half a million bucks and then run out of money before you could furnish it! How stupid can you be?" he stopped his diatribe and wiped the sweat off his brow with a huge handkerchief. "Look," he continued scanning the room with a mocking eye, "Not even a chair to sit on, and yet, the most expensive antique *piano!* And you can't even play it!"

"I can learn to play" Bob said meekly.

The man ignored him. "There's one more thing," he said. "I've arranged for the American Cowboy Magazine to do a big spread on you, pictures and all. I rented a beautiful horse for you to pose on, but I can't let the photographers come here, to this phony palace. You'll be a laughing stock! Your fans want to see you as a cowboy, as a *macho* man, do you understand?" He plumped himself on the floor, his back propped against the wall.

"What should I do, then? Tell me, you're my agent," Bob said with a sigh of resignation.

"Get rid of this house. That's first. Then, buy a ranch somewhere in the Valley, not too far from Hollywood. Stock the ranch with a few horses and some cattle. Then, we'll have *Life Magazine* do a cover story about you, not just a *fan* mag. We'll show you astride a horse, we'll write about your bravery during the war, show your medals and all that stuff. But get rid of this house and this French *thing*." He pointed at me with derision.

"It's not *a thing*, it is the most beautiful French piano!" Bob cried, his pride injured. "I always wanted to speak French and learn how to play piano, and after I had been to Paris during the war, I . . ."

"Snap out of it! We know, we know, you fell in love with everything *French!* I've heard it all before," the agent interrupted impatiently. "Go ahead, study your French and take piano lessons, but do it *quietly*. Understand? Your fans want to see you as a *cowboy*, a real *American cowboy*, as American as meat and potatoes, as American as the Fourth of July, as American as . . ."

"As apple pie," Bob added.

"Yeah! As American as *apple pie!*" the agent yelled at him. "You must work on this image of yours. Your fans want to see you on *the ranch*. They expect nothing else. I have a thousand fan letters to prove it!"

"Okay!" Bob shouted, angry at last. "Okay, I'll do it! I'll sell the house that I love and buy some stinking ranch! All my life I lived among the cows and barns and piles of manure . . . What do you know about country life? Have you ever gotten up before dawn to milk a cow or to feed some chickens? Have you ever shoveled manure after school to make a few bucks for a movie? Well, I have. And I had enough of it! I wanted to learn French, and to travel, and to read Encyclopedia Britannica, and to learn how to play a piano and, to play something better than *chopsticks*. I wanted to become *cultured!*"

"Hey, hey! *Culture-Smalture!* Hold it!" the agent laughed. "Don't be so passionate about your blasted *culture*. You still can do it all when you establish your image as a *cowboy!* Look at Gene Autry or Roy Rogers. Their images are so strong that even if they took up *knitting*, no one would bat an eye. But they are getting old. The country is ready for a *new* American cowboy—and you can be it. Don't miss your boat, boy. Wise up! When you become the *cowboy star*—you can learn every damned language in the world and play piccolo, and they would love it. But not yet. Not yet!"

"Okay," Bob said wearily. "You win. Put the house on the market and buy me a ranch. Only make sure that there will be someone to shovel the manure."

"But of course, *sweetheart*, I don't expect a big movie star like you to do barn chores. We'll hire a bunch of cow-hands, don't you worry."

"Can't I keep this piano? I can have it at the ranch," Bob pleaded.

"Nope. Your furnishings must be functional and simple. No decadent foreign antiques. Only simple American made furniture," the agent said.

"Okay, Irving, you've got the *carte blanche*."

"Oh, oh . . . No more French words. I don't even mind if you start saying *"ain't"* from time to time, but no more fancy *French* words!"

Bob sighed and stared at me with a bitter expression on his face. "I snatched this piano from my high school . . . Right after the war . . ." he said at last.

"You must act decisively. I'll arrange to sell it. It's worth a few grand. I know a couple of guys at the MGM and Fox studios. They'll go for this piano. What the hell, you'll make a few bucks on its sale!"

And so, I was sold. I was moved to the property department of a big movie studio, the mighty MGM. The warehouse where I was kept was a huge, barn-like structure, bursting with all kinds of furniture, lamps, musical instruments, rugs and tapestries, medieval armor, paintings and clocks. We were known collectively as the *props* and were stored accordingly. Thus, there were rows of pianos and harps, separate rows of tables and chairs, sofas and armoires. There were rows of mannequins in heavy armor, which stood like medieval knights shoulder to shoulder, their shields locked in an uneven phalanx. There were hundreds of mirrors, hung one next to another reflecting the stored items and creating the impression of a veritable, endless treasure trove. From time to time, some items would be temporary removed to take part in the filming of a motion picture.

Soon, I too, was called upon. I was to be in a movie taking place in Paris around 1890's.

As they wheeled me on the set, I felt that I had returned to my youth. The set looked exactly like Paris. Were it not for the supporting scaffolding of false walls or wired leaves on artificial trees and shrubs, I would have thought that I was back in Paris. I don't remember the plot of the picture, but it was really not important.

I made several pictures where the actors pretended to play piano. The camera angles were always such that their hands were never shown. Later, a professional pianist would play the required music and the cameras would concentrate on my keyboard and the pianist's hands. After some clever editing and splicing of the film, no one was able to distinguish between the fake and the real performance.

I enjoyed my studio work. I especially liked being a part of the musical picture *Gigi*. It was set in Paris during the so-called *La Belle Époque*. A charming French ballerina, Leslie Caron played the heroine Gigi. The film was full of marvelous songs that I continue to hear on the radio even to this day, songs such as "The Day They Invented Champagne," or "Thank Heaven for Little Girls," and others. It was a wonderful picture, with the colorful costumes of the period, slightly naughty in its story but not offensive in its depiction of Paris *demi-monde*. During the months of filming, *I felt that I was back in Paris*. Every piece of furniture reminded me of the handsome salon where the great Franz Liszt had touched my keys. It also reminded me of my first love, Solange de Matignon and her family.

Yes, I loved my studio work. In several pictures I was given an individual credit—*Pleyel Piano*, which made me a celebrity among my companions at the warehouse. Only three other pianos received similar honors: the magnificent concert grand Steinway, a baby grand Baldwin and a beautiful rosewood Chickering. The Chickering kept bragging about a letter from Franz Liszt' which was apparently kept in a display case at the Chickering piano factory in Boston. Liszt wrote that he had three wishes: to see an American prairie, to visit the Niagara Falls, and to play a Chickering piano!

I don't know how much truth there was in that little anecdote, but our Chickering was puffy with pride as if Liszt actually had meant *him*. I deflated the Chickering considerably when I told of my personal acquaintance with Liszt and for good measure, dropped a few other names, such as Debussy and Saint-Saëns. The Steinway, hearing our discussion, added fire to it by saying that Giacomo Puccini, the great opera composer, wrote a letter from which he quoted: *'Steinway is the best piano I've ever played'*. My neighbor, the Baldwin, joined the controversy, pointing with pride that our own Los Angeles Philharmonic Symphony advertised in its programs that their *official* piano was the Baldwin.

Cut down to size, the Chickering stopped bragging and for a while refused to acknowledge us, but soon his enmity was forgotten. He was chosen to appear in a picture with Olivia de Havilland, and once again peace was restored.

I was happy in my work. I liked the variety of pictures and the dedicated people who made them. I enjoyed the bright lights and frenetic sounds and commotion before the director would call "Camera . . . Action . . ." and everyone would freeze in his tracks.

The plots of the films and the faces of the actors merged for me into a multi-colored kaleidoscope, which I found stimulating. I went from picture to picture, meeting the greatest stars such as Clark Gable, Bette Davis, Henry Fonda, Joan Crawford and many others. Ingrid Bergman became my favorite, perhaps because she was a European, as I was. I kept falling in love with all the ladies as usual, despite my advanced age. Then, one day, I met Bob Wright again.

In the several years that had passed, he had become a famous movie star. He recognized me at once. He patted me fondly, ran a finger in a long *glissando* over my keyboard and then quickly turned away. I knew that he did not want anyone to notice his emotions of meeting me again. I sensed that he had loved and missed me.

Bob was to appear in a movie where he played the part of a tough sheriff and I was supposed to be the piano in a gambling saloon on a riverboat. A strange feeling of "*déjà vu*" seized me when I was wheeled on the set. It looked exactly like the saloon on the *Daisy-Lou*! It had garish red and gold appointments, the same heavy opulence. Except that the walls were paneled in painted plywood, instead of genuine mahogany. "If they only knew that I had been on a *real* riverboat!" I thought.

Bob was to have a violent scene where he had to fight several bad men. I observed with interest as his stand-in, a stuntman, made spectacular leaps and falls as he fought with his adversaries. Bob watched, seated comfortably in a chair with his name on it. He was too valuable a star to risk a smashed nose or a broken rib. It was wise, I thought. Then I noticed that I, too, had a stand-in! A piano made of plywood, but an exact replica of me, down to the last detail. "What are they going to do with this mock instrument?" I thought. Soon I knew. At one point in the fight, the hero, trying to escape, was to push the piano across the room, pinning his enemies against the wall and escaping through the window. As the piano was crushed at the wall, a lighted candle that was standing on its case had to overturn, and start the fire that burned down the saloon and, of course, the piano.

I watched the scene being rehearsed again and again, until every moment was synchronized to perfection. It flattered my vanity that I had my own stand-in and that the director realized that I was too valuable to be exposed to unnecessary risks. Weeks later I saw the same scene on the screen during the celebration on the set. I could not tell the difference between Bob and the stuntman or, come to think of it, between my stand-in and me.

Even though I loved my work at the studio, I could not help but think that I was really wasted. I was used as a *prop* to create the background for a story, but rarely to make music, which was my real function. Deep in my heart I yearned to be owned again by some young person, like Bernard or Claude Debussy, who would cherish me for what I was, a *superb musical instrument* and not a piece of expensive antique furniture. I longed to be *exercised* daily, like a fine car on a freeway, allowed to go at full speed, or a racehorse at the track, spurred to the height of its ability. My keys needed to be touched by a true musician, who would make me burst forth with dramatic or lyrical sound, who would make the scales and arpeggios race, following one note after another in fast succession.

I tried to find some satisfaction in being an *antique* piano. Occasionally I was invited to brighten up a party at the studio to celebrate a completed movie. The producers would want to have some *class* and I would be the one to provide it. Actors, directors and cameramen, carpenters and electricians would gather on the set among the phony walls and painted scenery. The producers would make speeches, congratulating themselves and the others, predicting the Academy Awards, stroking each other's vanity. There would be tables laden with food and drinks and a small condo band playing popular tunes. A studio pianist would be banging on my keys, but I didn't mind. I was making *music*.

At one of such studio parties, I met Marilyn Monroe. I promptly fell in love with her blond, helpless beauty. Although she was not the star of the movie that we were celebrating, she instantly became the star of the party. Everyone tried to get close to her, to talk to her, to touch her or listen with attention to her soft, breathy voice. But I was the luckiest of all. Someone asked Marilyn to sing. After some hesitation, she agreed. She lowered the lid of my case and asked to be lifted on my top. She sat there, in her tight silver lamé dress held over her shoulders by invisible straps. She sang a popular number from her film *Gentlemen Prefer Blondes* in her small, childlike voice. I did not hear the words. Nor did I care. I was just overwhelmed with happiness to be near the divine creature that was Marilyn Monroe.

Since that night I had a secret dream, to be in the same picture with her. Alas, my dream had never been fulfilled. Although I had seen her at the parties and even accompanied her several more times, I never really had a chance to *know* her. As I learned some years later, no one *knew* her, really. Beautiful, tragic Marilyn had died by her own hand. I was deeply grieved. I wished that I could have paid my final respects to this lovely unhappy girl, but of course, it was out of the question. I was only a piano.

I continued to appear in films, but I began to notice that the mood and the style of Hollywood were changing. There were new young faces among the actors and a new trend of making movies abroad. We, the *props* at the huge warehouses, spent more time in gathering dust than working. Soon, instead of twenty or thirty pictures being in production simultaneously, there were only a dozen or less. Actors began to form their own production companies to compete with the big studios. Television, this new form of art became very popular and it too, entered the serious competition for the viewing audiences. Year after year passed with fewer films produced by the giant studios. I heard that Bob Wright had at last shed his *cowboy image* and created his own independent company. He produced and directed several films where he also acted and, to everyone's surprise, emerged speaking French in one of the pictures. I fantasized that he may still remember me and would want to have me back, but . . . it did not happen.

The boredom in our warehouse was becoming unbearable. Then, to our astonishment, we heard that the MGM decided to sell all its *props* and costumes at a great public auction. We knew that for years the studios had been unloading their land holdings. The best example was Century City—a modern steel and glass metropolis that sprung up on the former lot of the 20th Century-Fox studios. Now the studios were going one step further, they were selling their vast accumulations of costumes, furniture, antiques and musical instruments.

Once again I was forced to face a change in my destiny. "Who is going to bid for me at this fantastic sale?" I wondered. "What further adventures are ahead of me?" I thought as I waited with anxious curiosity for the date of the auction.

Long before the announced date, May 1970 (to think of it, almost exactly a hundred years since I was first introduced to the world!) a firm of international auctioneers began its preparations for the big sale. There were rumors among us that the whole lot was already bought for a mere one and a half million dollars by the auctioneers themselves, who had planned to resell us for many times more, betting on the public crave for movie nostalgia. We were photographed and tagged, and our pictures and descriptions appeared in glossy journals around the world. A special catalogue was printed and it instantly became a collector's item. Some wit coined a *bon mot* that the auction will have "*Everything on the block but the Lion's roar,*" alluding to the famous MGM logo.

For three weeks Stage 27 was swamped with hundreds of buyers and on-lookers, who had paid the stiff admission price of one hundred dollars to be present at this historic sale.

The air around me buzzed with hysterical excitement. There was talk that Judy Garland's ruby-red shoes from *The Wizard of Oz* could bring *fifteen thousand dollars*, or a simple gingham dress from the same picture, at least a thousand dollars! The prospective bidders milled around us, touching, poking, reading the descriptions in their catalogues, many smiling as they recognized some items from films seen a long time ago and remembered with fondness. There were more than *three hundred and fifty thousand* items from more than two thousand movies made during the past fifty-six years.

All these statistics staggered one's imagination. People acted as if they were intoxicated. They paid enormous sums for items not worth more than a few dollars only because some movie star had held it in his or her hands or wore it in some famous picture. They were betting and buying Roman chariots and wooden eggcups, railroad coaches and oil portraits. They competed for eighteenth century costumes and medieval armor.

My attention was soon centered on a group of people who were particularly interested in antique furniture. From their conversation I presumed that they were the curators of some museum. They tried to bid for a set of the *authentic* Louis XIV furniture, which was used by Norma Shearer in her film *Marie-Antoinette*. However, a pretty little blond, a current movie star, Debbie Reynolds, blocked them. A rumor quickly spread among us that Debbie Reynolds bought the four pieces for 1,200 dollars, not for herself but for a projected Hollywood Hall of Fame, which was her *idée fixe*. She was negotiating for a lot of memorabilia and we all wished that she would buy all of us. We the antiques, we belonged in the Hall of Fame.

At night, when all the crowds were gone, we exchanged our impressions of the passed days. Everyone hoped to be bought by Debbie Reynolds for the Hollywood museum. Like people, we sought comfort in the familiar company of each other. To be scattered around the country did not appeal to us. As for me, I had a different ambition. I did not want to stand behind a velvet rope in a museum; I longed to be bought by someone who would appreciate me for what I was—a superb piano. Frankly, I hoped that Debbie Reynolds would buy me for *herself*. She was exceptionally pretty and I must admit, my heart was pounding whenever I gazed at her lovely, clean-cut beauty.

Destiny interfered in the next *étape* of my life, fulfilling my most fervent desire.

For several days I watched the same group of three women and two men who spent all of their time around the musical instruments. One of the women must have been a concert pianist, for whenever she tried the instruments, she exhibited the high technical knowledge, confidence and professional ability of one who was accustomed to playing in public. She sat in front of me and played the first movement of Beethoven's *Sonata in F minor opus 57*, the so-called *Appassionata*. It was the first time since I played it with Claude Debussy for the pleasure of Madame von Meck. Now, I played it again, with all the passion I could muster. The pianist and I were rewarded with spontaneous applause of the auction goers.

"Who are these people?" we asked one another that night. The mystery was solved the next day. The group that was interested in musical instruments was called *Friends of Music* and it represented a philanthropic organization associated with one of the great Universities.

"Oh, to be bought by them!" I thought, fired up by a possibility of finding myself in the quiet academic atmosphere, helping once again some deserving young person to reach the pinnacle of perfection, as I had done it with my dear Claude Debussy.

My dream did come true. At the next day auction, *Friends of Music* had bid for me and bought me for a bargain price. I said *adieu* to my competitors, the *Chickering* and the *Baldwin* as the auction helpers loaded me on the truck. The *Chickering* and the *Baldwin* vibrated their strings wishing me good luck in my new career in the academic circles. My best friend at the studio, the concert grand *Steinway* was already sold to a prominent psychiatrist Dr. George Wayne, a *connoisseur* of music and other fine things in life. His good friend, pianist Oscar Levant, who had often appeared in MGM great musical films, recommended that Dr. Wayne buy the *Steinway*. "I'll play Gershwin's *Rhapsody in Blue* for you at your next party," Oscar Levant promised.

I used to envy the *Steinway* his great repertoire of American music. I was better suited for European romantic music, I thought, even though I was quite good at playing jazz. But now, the new horizons were opening before me. Perhaps, I'll finally appear at some great concert hall with a big symphony orchestra, as I always wished to do but was never able to, being a *private piano*.

I was taken across the city over the frightening freeways right into the quiet practice room on the campus of the University where the *Friends of Music* were waiting for me.

"This is a marvelous stroke of luck!" exclaimed one of them, a grandmotherly lady. "At last we found an instrument that will fit our high purpose!"

The members of the group watched as I was unwrapped from protective padded blankets and placed in the center of the practice room. "All we have to do now is to leave our *Pleyel* in the capable hands of our tuner!" The grandmotherly lady bowed to a man whom I noticed at the auction as one of the most demanding of our prospective buyers. He was the famous piano tuner.

"Let's toast our new friend, *Monsieur Pleyel!*" exclaimed one of the younger men of the group. "I brought some champagne!" he reached into his backpack for a bottle of *La Veuve Cliquot*. "We have no glasses, but I hope you don't mind paper cups. They are in the hall at the water cooler!"

"To *Monsieur Pleyel!*" They all laughed, toasting me with French champagne in paper cups.

In a few days I was thoroughly cleaned, polished and tuned. I was wheeled on the stage of the University Concert Hall. The members of the Music Department minutely examined me inside and out. They all played snatches of Bach, Tchaikovsky or Beethoven, or simply ran arpeggios and struck a few chords. I could see that they *loved* what they heard.

"Congratulations to our *Friends of Music*," exclaimed the Dean of the Music Department. "You discovered a gem! Let's try it at the recital next week with Jim Parker!"

"Next week?" I thought, "In a *real* Concert Hall, with a *real* pianist?" My feet turned cold under me.

Next week the Concert Hall was full of students, teachers, and music lovers. My *real* pianist turned out to be a fourteen-years-old prodigy, Jim Parker from Watts. He was a thin black young man, very serious and gentle. I worked with him for several days rehearsing a well-chosen program of Chopin and Scriabin, a Russian composer unknown to me. I had heard Alexander Scriabin's name at Madame von Meck's salon but I had never heard his music until young Jim introduced me to it. Scriabin's music was full of passion, much too serious for such a young man as Jim, yet, the boy played him brilliantly, choosing one of Scriabin's own favorite works—Sonata #7 *in F-sharp major, Opus 64.*

My heart was bursting with pride as I waited for the young virtuoso. He entered the stage, frail and shy, wearing a turtleneck sweater, his spectacles catching the bright reflections of the spotlight. His hair was combed in an Afro style that I noticed was popular among young black men and girls. The audience met him with thunderous applause. Apparently the listeners were well acquainted with his great talent. I felt ecstatic. At last I was to perform in a *Concert Hall!*

The boy began to play. He grabbed the bull by its horns, so to speak, by starting with Scriabin's Sonata. I knew that Jim could handle Scriabin. As for me, I was back in my true element, classical music, collaborating with a talented young musician, who reminded me of my beloved Claude.

The audience called the young man back again and again, demanding an encore after encore. I knew that Jim was exhausted, as was I, but he played a Chopin's mazurka and since the concert specifically consisted of French and Russian music, he played several short Tchaikovsky's pieces, each describing a different month of the year.

Brought back again, Jim finished the concert with the Debussy's *"Clair de Lune"*. I thought it was a good omen: Debussy was with me again, inaugurating a new prodigy for me to guide and to nourish.

The concert was over. The Hall emptied. The members of the *Friends of Music* gathered around Jim and me.

"Well, how did you like the sound of our *Monsieur Pleyel?*" the grandmotherly lady asked him.

"I loved it. I think it is the finest piano in the whole world!" he exclaimed. Everyone applauded. I wished I could take a bow, but all I could do was to grin with all my eighty-eight teeth.

"You were wonderful!" the old lady said. "But you must be tired now. Your parents are waiting to take you home." Jim bade good-bye to his admirers and left with his parents. Talking among themselves, the *Friends of Music* left the Hall. The lights were turned off. I was alone. But I did not feel lonely. I knew that I would play the important part in developing young talents. I would be doing what I always loved, that is, working with young people and creating great music.

What a wonderful future for someone, who was well into his *second* century, yet was still able to be of service!